QUEEN DAFFODIL'S DEMISE

JOHN BUSH

johnbush03@icloud.com

979-8-9907787-1-9

DEDICATION

This book is dedicated to our dear friend and fellow New Bohemian, Brad Houser, who passed away July 24th, 2023. Brad was always extremely interested in whatever I was writing. He, maybe more than anyone, always encouraged me and made me believe that I could do this. "You can do this," he'd say to me. "You've got stories in you; you've got stories to tell." Then, he'd laugh that staccato laugh of his, snort, and nod affirmatively. Anyone who knew Brad knew that he didn't hand out compliments lightly. If Brad Houser told you something, he meant it. Brad putting faith in me gave me faith in myself. Thanks Brad, for all the love and good times we've shared. Your badassness is still reverberating in the cosmos, motivating and inspiring everyone who knew you.

This book is also dedicated to Bobby Jack Pack. Bobby was a good friend and a super talented multimedia artist. He was a painter, photographer, and videographer. He wrote, filmed, and directed his own television series for local cable television in the 1990s called *The Bobby Jack Pack Show*. It was a brilliant show shot on film before digital cameras. It was a montage of short non-sequitur pieces edited together. It was a painstaking process that took hours of editing, but the results were amazing. The show was hilarious. Bobby was an inspiration to many people, including myself. He was a renegade – so talented at everything he did and always good for a laugh. We had the good fortune of driving across the country together in 1993 when I was moving to Seattle. That is another story all unto itself…

FOREWORD

"We pray that peoples of all faiths, all races, all nations, may have their great human needs satisfied; that those now denied opportunity shall come to enjoy it to the full; that all who yearn for freedom may experience its spiritual blessings; that those who have freedom will understand, also, its heavy responsibilities; that all who are insensitive to the needs of others will learn charity; that the scourges of poverty, disease and ignorance will be made to disappear from the earth, and that, in the goodness of time, all peoples will come to live together in a peace guaranteed by the binding force of mutual respect and love."

-President Dwight D. Eisenhower's farewell address, January 17th, 1961.

TABLE OF CONTENTS

CHARACTER LIST
(IN ORDER OF APPEARANCE)

Ryder
Betty
Carl
The girl with the rose petal voice
Crystal and Grace
The urchins
The lanky boy of 14
Crystal's mom, Pam
The twins in braided pigtails
Coyote
Noah Billingsworth
Queen Daffodil
Joshua & Jeremiah Moynihan
Gus Gutridge and Mrs. Gutridge
Tabatha and Mary Beth
Paraffin
General Gaughinlas
General Carwrimes
Skeeter
Junior Jr. III
Norman & Orville Poff
Elizer
Nora
Afonja
Raiyn
Colonel Wallerstein
Lieutenant Pablo Steinberg
Marcus Junius

CHAPTER ONE

The mind had temporarily turned to sand. The air was full of pollutants and the weather was grey like the color of death. Ryder recalled a time on a carefree summer Sunday when grandmother was alive. She had come into town for a visit to the dilapidated old house on Live Oak Street. The house wasn't much to look at, but it was home. There were no longer live oaks or any other type of tree in the city. Humanity now scavenged for water and food in order to survive.

Ryder rode through the streets on a bicycle. Desperate and destitute individuals regarded the two-wheeled vehicle as a sign of wealth. People were filthy, their dirty hands and fingers begged for food, crumbs, anything to survive. Ryder, not afraid of eye contact, waved them on. Society survived on starvation pills doled out by the government, along with water purification tablets that made the water safe to drink. Even after applying the purification tablets, the water appeared chalky, proving difficult to stomach. Fresh water – the kind you could see through – was a rarity.

Straddling an old mountain bike pieced together from salvaged parts of several broken bicycles, Ryder scanned the surroundings, smelled the air, and swallowed the last gulp of water from a plastic bottle found behind a row of dumpsters. Next to the plastic bottle was a folded-up piece of parchment paper containing the remaining crust from a loaf of bread. Ryder was starving and couldn't believe the good fortune in finding a real piece of food. Carefully unwrapping the parchment paper that held the delicate find, Ryder savored the stale morsels, letting them dissolve slowly in the mouth. Saving a small piece of bread, Ryder gently offered the last bite to a stray mutt that was sniffing about. The dog was a frightful sight and was very cautious of people. He didn't want to come any closer to Ryder than he already was.

"Come here, little fellow. I won't hurt you," Ryder said.

The dog turned his head and stood up to pace. He was curious yet afraid of the human. The mutt had seen several of his mates captured and killed for food; he didn't want to become someone else's prey. But he was also starving, and this looked like food the person was offering him. The stray sniffed the air.

Ryder continued to gently coax the pup by saying, "Come

on, boy, come on. I won't hurt you."

The dog eased his way over a little closer. Bit by bit, inch by inch, the mangy stray scooched his way closer to the human, eventually standing only an arm's length away. Ryder held out the piece of bread, touching it to the dog's snout, who politely licked it into his mouth, inhaling it in less than two wags of his tail. Ryder gave the little dog a couple of scratches behind the ears before putting both feet on the pedals then steering the bike into the direction of the steam rising off the desolate city streets that lay ahead. As if blissfully floating through a world with no problems, Ryder rode through the streets without a care. Mind clear, no thoughts of the past or worries of the future, just in the present moment. Riding.

Alone on the melancholy biped, a self-propelling time machine, Ryder's thoughts turned to finding grease for the bicycle's chain. Cruising down the quiet, lonely streets through the polluted fog, Ryder could make out the long, dark outline of people stretching around the block of a barren warehouse. Blank stares were plastered on every face as folks queued up for starvation pills. Starvation pills were handed out by the government to stave off hunger. A pill to cure thirst had not yet been developed. Scientists were hard at work, not allowing their failures to prevent them from trying repeatedly.

Ash and soot covered all of the cars, as well as the pavement, buildings, people's faces, and their clothes. Sunny days were, at best, nothing more than a grey, sometimes silver glow that frosted its way through the atmosphere fighting to be let out, like a newborn clawing its way through the birth canal, clutching at life just trying to be seen, to be born.

Ryder pedaled past the line of gloom, ignoring the drudge, and stopping at the front of the line. Sitting behind an old metal school desk was a large muscular woman, looking fierce with a shaved head and tattoos on her massive arms. She had tiny, pushed-up nostrils that resembled those of a pug.

"Hey, Betty. I gotta see Carl."

"Goddamn it, Ryder! Carl ain't here," she gruffly replied.

The question seemed to anger Betty even more than she already appeared to be. Her puffy fingers turned white as she clutched the wooden handle of a rubber stamp tightly in her grip. Slapping it on an ink pad and stamping it on the boney hands of two of the people waiting in line, she then motioned for the peasants to go inside the tent. Being careful not to touch anyone's skin, nurses in masks and gloves popped the pills into the open mouths of the peasants, all of whom had skin the color of concrete.

Betty gritted her teeth and whispered, "Don't make me say this out loud, but I think Carl has been deloused."

'Deloused' was the term used when citizens were secretly removed from society. Rumors ran amok; however, the common thought was that people who were deloused were chopped up into tiny bits in experiments in extermination then subsequently used in attempts to produce topsoil for growing food.

"I gotta find Carl. He's got grease for my chain."

"Look, Ryder. Don't come 'round here no more talking about such foolishness. You're liable to get us all killed. Go on now. Get going. I can't be seen talking to you."

Betty slammed the rubber stamp onto the ink pad then onto three more boney hands. She wrinkled her pug nose and gave Ryder a dirty look before giving a quick sideways nod to get away. Thinking it wise to take Betty's advice, Ryder rode on, trying not to draw any attention to either of them.

Pedaling down the vacant roads, strange sounds were emanating from the empty streets and alleys. The wind, with its subtle changes, moaned and howled, causing the lids from empty dumpsters to squeak and move slightly, as if waking from a long slumber, their creaking giving warnings of hell. 'Stranger beware, or they will get you, too', they seemed to beckon. A lone halogen streetlamp flickered and crackled. From the shadows, a hooded figure appeared, clad in a brown twine robe. Despite the dangers and not being able to clearly make out a face, Ryder felt compelled to stop.

The hooded figure approached seemingly without fear. Gliding directly in front of Ryder, she stopped. She spoke in a delicate voice – a voice as soft and fragile as petals of a rose.

She said, "I am on a linear track."

She paused and looked from side to side before repeating herself.

"I am on a linear track. You are a wavelength. Our paths will only cross at certain junctures."

Ryder began to speak, but the woman interrupted, "You

must know when to stay silent and when to ask questions."

The hooded figure held a finger to her shadowed mouth then bowed her head, shielding her face by the shadow of her hood. Listening carefully to her surroundings, she backed away slowly. While doing so, she stretched out her arms, batting them like a bird in slow motion, vanishing backwards into the shadows.

Ryder straddled the bike while remaining silent and wondered if what just happened was real or a short circuit in the brain. Starved from hunger, perhaps it was another nourishment-deprived hallucination. The hair on the back of the neck stood on end. The distant echo of hard-soled shoes and the murmur of voices sent Ryder standing up straight in the saddle. With the grace of a creature in the wild, Ryder rode away, eventually evaporating into the steam of the darkening streets.

CHAPTER TWO

Night fell on the coast where Crystal and her companion, Grace, lived. *This is an exciting time*, Crystal thought to herself. In the distance, she could hear the sounds of The People's workers clearing debris with their machinery. She noticed the air beginning to clear, sweet with the faint smell of freshness. The scent of trees…perhaps they were cedars or evergreens of some kind. She could smell their sweetness cutting through the acidic soot of the polluted air. Most days, the air was like breathing in the taste of battery acid. The hint of fresh air made her cheeks flush with excitement. She smiled. It was a sign that some forms of life had survived, and that the resistance and the cleaning efforts of The People's People were having an effect.

CHAPTER THREE

Ryder rode all night, farther away from the city than ever before. Peering through the fog early the next morning, Ryder barely noticed the gentle movement of deer quietly following a path worn down by generations of animals and draining water from centuries ago. Moving through the fog like Bedouins or a tribe of indigenous people, the starved and depleted animals traveled silently through the misty canyon in search of anything to eat.

The morning fog crept along the slopes, following the curves of the earth as it began to clear. A giant silhouette could be seen through the clearing far off in the trees. There were massive cone-shaped pillars outlining the top of the pointy, sloped roof of a gothic-style mansion. Ryder carried the bike over thick brush and overgrowth, forging a path as straight as possible toward the darkened structure. Walking deep into a canyon, the mansion fell out of sight. Using landmarks for dead reckoning, Ryder found the way – crisscrossing back and forth up the slopes of the steep canyon, lugging the mountain bike to the top of the ridge until the magnificent, abandoned estate was in view.

Out of breath and not wanting to be careless, Ryder waited at the edge of the forest and paid close attention by watching, listening, and making certain that no one, not another living soul or beast, could be inside or anywhere near the dilapidated mansion. After crouching and waiting for about 30 minutes, Ryder sat back against the bike and waited another half hour, just to be extra cautious. Relaxing, Ryder drifted off into a light sleep, waking every now and again whenever the wind blew or a fly whizzed by.

Once fully awake and surmising the situation, it was time to take a risk. Ryder pushed the bike through the wispy weeds and walked across the once-opulently manicured grounds leading up to the weathered remains of a bygone and glorious architectural creation. Slowly circling the perimeter and finally reaching the backside of the estate, behind the decrepit 10-foot-tall hedgerows was a sight Ryder hadn't seen in over three years: a flock of birds. Songbirds mostly – cardinals, sparrows, blue jays, and wrens, mixed with pigeons and grackles. They were feeding off bits of things in the dirt and drinking water from a filthy swimming pool. Grown over with moss, the pool was only a quarter full of water. Debris floating in the quagmire gave the birds plenty of options to perch on as they dipped their beaks and wings into the earthy liquid. Ryder took a stick, swirled it around in the murky water, and opened up a clearing before lowering a quart bottle down into its wetness by using a rope that was tied and taped to the neck of the plastic bottle. Hoisting up the bottle and popping two extra strength purifying tablets into the dirty water, Ryder screwed the lid on tight and shook the bottle vigorously for several minutes before tying the rope back through a belt loop. In just over an hour, the gooey, green sludge would be safe to drink. Difficult to stomach, it would be milky white and taste like chalk, but it would be hydration.

Staring at things floating in the pool and losing focus on the surroundings, Ryder failed to notice the group of children and adolescents gathering outside at the back of the house. Most of them were barefoot with shabby clothes, raggedy hair, gnarly teeth, and dirty skin, almost green with filth. Unkempt and unwashed, the juveniles moved and acted like a pack, surviving on pure animal instincts. Surveying the intruder and assessing the risks, they crept forward. With inquisitive curiosity, as if seeing something for the very first time, they approached Ryder while remaining at a safe distance.

Trying not to overreact once becoming aware of the urchins, Ryder raised a hand slowly to greet them.

"Hello. How's it going? Do you live here?"

The barefooted scamps, most of them shirtless (even the girls), began making chirping sounds similar to squirrels.

They turned their heads from side to side, examining Ryder's size, the bike, the clothes, the bottle of water. They were bewildered and in awe of what stood before them.

"Can you guys help me? I need to find grease for my chain. Do you have any supplies, food, or oils I could use on my chain? I can trade you pills. I have purification tablets and some lower-dose starvation pills."

Ryder mentioned the starvation pills in a whisper since they were government issued and illegal to carry away from the clinics. The squirrel chatter escalated, and Ryder's stomach began to feel uneasy. Ryder thought about asking again for grease for the bicycle chain, but instead decided to start backing away slowly. Looking up at the mansion, Ryder began counting windows…about 25 or 30 lined the outside walls. Interested to see what was inside, the hairs on the back of the neck stood on end. The crowd of grimy kids was moving toward Ryder, who wondered if one should act casual or quickly flee. The chirping sounds were getting louder and more intense until a single voice screamed.

"Enough!"

Silence fell over the manor grounds. The starkness sent a shiver-inducing chill down Ryder's spine.

"This is for you," said a lanky 14-year-old boy, who stepped forward from the crowd. He approached Ryder and held a rolled-up scroll that was wrapped with a piece of white gauze. The boy was easily seven inches taller than any of the other children. He had ears he hadn't yet grown into. The ears stood out flat, pointing away from his head like two solar panels on a satellite. He walked with his shoulders slumped forward. It appeared he didn't have good balance, but his large feet kept him from falling over flat on his face. He avoided eye contact.

The boy stiffly stretched out his arm and clutched the scroll firmly, being mindful not to crush it. Holding it out in front of himself, he repeated, "Here, this is for you."

Ryder looked surprised. "For me? What is it?"

The slender boy didn't answer. He turned and slumped away back into the crowd. The chirping sounds resumed, but at a more subdued level. Ryder removed the gauze ring and unfolded the scroll. It contained the following phrase and drawing:

I am on a linear track.
You are a wavelength.
Our paths will only cross at certain junctures.

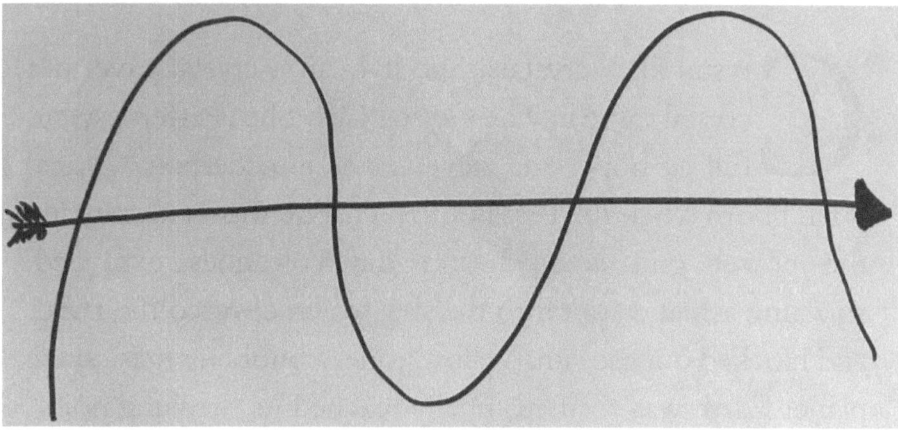

CHAPTER FOUR

Crystal likes crystals. She lives in a crystal cave in a crystal mine in The Crystal City. She is effervescent, full of hope, and never gives into despair. Crystal wasn't born when the first bombs fell. She wasn't alive when the power grid crashed and the volcanoes exploded, shooting ash and soot into the sky, which covered the Earth and blocked out the sun. Yellowstone, a bubbling mass since planet Earth was formed, finally reached its breaking point, sending fiery lava and ash into the atmosphere. It destroyed a huge portion of The United States. It affected the entire global weather system, which ultimately caused chaos and destruction to mankind and nature on a worldwide scale.

Crystal's mom, Pam, was a survivor. Pam's dad (Crystal's grandpa) was an expert in ores and the mining industries. All but one of Crystal's uncles died in the mines. She didn't know any of them except the youngest one, Jeremiah. Crystal never knew her own father. Pam barely knew the man either. Their love was a passionate one-night stand. He was a roving miner briefly passing through town.

When the heavy-handed government, led by the evil doings of Queen Daffodil, turned into a full-fledged military state, Pam fled, taking Crystal and her little brother, Jonah, to the safety of a hidden commune located in a crystal mine that The People's People called 'The Crystal City'. On a stormy evening, they left in an old, beat-up brown Chevy Impala station wagon. The thing barely started and ran just long enough to get them out of the city without being discovered, killed, or tortured. They finished their journey on foot, arriving at a location known amongst a lucky few as a meeting place where the good people of The Crystal City would shuttle families to the safety of the city.

The station wagon they escaped in belonged to a wannabe boyfriend of her mom's, Nathaniel. Even as a young child, Crystal knew Nathaniel was a creep. Years later, she realized that although he was a creep, he did the right thing and saved her and her mom's life that fateful evening of the escape. Nate was an alcoholic and addicted to the government's starvation pills, which were basically a high-powered amphetamine loaded with vitamins, and a malt byproduct. When the higher potency starvation pills were abused, people with the addictive gene, like Nathaniel, became a sketched-out version of their former selves. Nate often exhibited scabs and open sores from compulsively scratching at the freckles that dotted his boney arms and sunken face.

Nate's brother, Daniel, was more stable and a much better person. Even though he and Pam never dated, he was the only caretaker and father figure in Crystal's life. Daniel drove the station wagon west of Delacroix with Crystal and her mom while Nathaniel stayed behind, causing a distraction by leading the authorities to his own whereabouts so that Crystal and her mom could escape the city unnoticed. Nate and his friends were captured and beaten before being executed. Machine gunned in their backs then buried in a shallow grave...their bodies burnt to a crisp, along with the house where they once lived.

Pam and Daniel were never romantic, but he helped take care of them and became a solid role model for Crystal. Crystal was enamored with him. Even more importantly, she always felt safe with Daniel; this gave her confidence she carried throughout her life.

This particular morning was special, and Crystal was full of hope. The efforts by The People's People were beginning to pay off. She could literally taste it in the air. That sweet smell, just a tiny hint of fresh air. Even the morning dew on the large leaves of the plants on her porch had the clear look and taste of water, as opposed to the acidic moisture that until recently, was the norm for precipitation. Hopefully, the past would change into a better future...if they could continue to regain the ecosystem by growing plants and changing the atmosphere so clean water could fall from the skies once again.

CHAPTER FIVE

Ryder's initial instinct was to ride away. The sun was beginning to set. The filthy, chirping children no longer posed a threat; instead, they had turned their backs and began dispersing into the evening woods. Some of them crawled into and underneath hedgerows. Several huddled into burrows, mounds of earth covered in thatched roofs with smoke holes at their crests for the cooking fires on the inside. Others climbed trees and into something resembling nests more than treehouses – more like tree huts. Homemade lanterns lit the humble dwellings made of meager wood flooring with tents and lean-tos derived from bark, twine, dried leaves, mud, and broken limbs. Seeing the crude lanterns piqued Ryder's interest. They must have oil to burn or some sort of substitute for grease if they have these lanterns.

After much deliberation, Ryder chose to stay, cautiously entering the dilapidated mansion. Most of the windows were no longer intact, broken, or missing the glass completely. Not trusting to leave the bicycle outside, Ryder carefully walked in, pushing the bike slowly through the ramshackle entryway, down barren hallways and large open, messy rooms. The rooms were mostly void of anything, minus bits of garbage and a few pallets on the floors in some of the rooms. There were no furnishings or items of any kind. It appeared there was an inadequate number of pallets for the number of adolescents seen milling about. Ryder and the bike didn't go unnoticed, yet no one spoke. Everyone parted the path, stepping out of the way as Ryder ambled through the hallways, peering into (and sometimes walking through) random rooms. Some of the rooms were magnificent in size, yet worn down to the dried-up skeletons of what they once were. There were rooms of many shapes and sizes leading into one another – small and cozy while others were large, cathedral-sized chambers. A few of the rooms were adorned with ornate wallpaper that had somehow survived the test of time, water damage, and/or vandalism.

After an arduous journey through a maze of dimly-lit rooms and hallways, Ryder approached two enormous open doorways of the grandest room of them all. An orange glow from a giant fireplace flickered down a pitch-black hallway; the hearth was easily 25 yards away from the doorway. The fireplace crackled with flames fueled from busted-up furniture and piles upon piles of books. Some of the books were bound in leather. Through the haze, Ryder recognized the tall, lanky boy along with two sisters – twins – in braided pigtails. Ryder didn't notice the twins earlier, but they were following the thin boy when he had handed out the scroll with the cryptic message.

The fireplace was a magnificent piece of architecture. In spite of the disrepair the rest of the mansion had fallen prey to, the fireplace hearth was pristine. It was carved in stone and inlaid with dark mahogany wood carvings depicting ancient Greek gods entwined with demons and naked angels. Nymphs frolicking and feeding one another in a woven and carved tale of immaculate detail remained mostly unharmed and in exquisite condition. The fireplace was as tall as four large men standing on each other's shoulders and as wide as 20 bicycles placed end to end. Handcrafted bookshelves lined the adjacent walls of the hearth, tall enough to rise far above the heads of giants. It took a moment for Ryder's eyes to adjust to the flickering firelight in the darkness, but it eventually became clear what one was looking at.

Books. Books upon books upon books. Rows and rows of books rising so high, one had to strain their neck to look upwards…and still, you couldn't see the ceiling or where the bookshelves ended. The books lined the walls all the way up to the endless sky of the room.

Ryder noticed that some of the shelves were empty. A small group of children was feeding the fire using three piles of books. Each child was no more than nine or 10 years old.

They moved at a hypnotic pace, never saying a word, staring at the flames with the brainless look of zombies. Besides the pile of books, the children were also breaking up antique furniture and tossing the broken pieces into the inferno. As the pile of furniture diminished, more would be brought in. Old chairs, tables, and dressers were stacked in carts and dumped into a heap. The same happened with the books. Wheelbarrows full of books were brought in from different parts of the building then emptied into the piles before being tossed in whole by children, some as young as seven and eight years old.

Transfixed by the methodical assemblage taking place, Ryder was unaware of a fit, shirtless person wearing a silk robe and colorful linen pants. He had entered the room a short time earlier. He wore a leather helmet, the kind worn centuries ago by tank commanders. The helmet, originally brown or olive green, had been painted fluorescent orange. He wore leather work boots that were painted baby blue. In his mouth was a toothpick, which he didn't seem to be happy with, constantly rearranging its position between his lips. He was much older than the other kids, probably closer to 18 years old. The two made eye contact as the boy approached Ryder.

"How may I help you? My name is Coyote."

Ryder was at a loss for words. Coyote looked annoyed.

"What do you want?" the boy asked sharply.

When Ryder didn't answer, Coyote repeated what he had said. This time, with force, pausing between each word.

"What, do, you, want?"

Finally, Ryder was able to speak. "How long have you lived here?"

Coyote didn't answer.

"Do you have a food source? I could really use something to eat. I also need to get some grease for my chain. I'm concerned about the rust in the gears and on the chain. I don't want it to ever seize up or break."

Coyote leaned over a bit to examine Ryder's bike. Looking up and down at the situation, he stared hard, dead into Ryder's eyes.

He then asked point blank, "What faction are you with?"

Coyote stood up straight and kept talking. "You're obviously not with the regime. Are you a government runaway? Are you on the run from a government job? Because if you are, I need to know right now. I can't harbor a fugitive. Harboring fugitives could get us in a lot of trouble or killed if we were to be found out. Are you being followed? Is there anyone after you? Speak the truth. I can spot a liar. And I don't suffer fools lightly."

"No, I don't work for the government or anybody else, for that matter. My entire family died from the plague or disappeared under very mysterious circumstances. They might've been deloused. I could no longer take the despair of the city, so I rode off unnoticed. Even if it kills me, I'm hoping to find something good out here. Anything has to be better than living the slow death of starvation or disease that awaits most people who live in the city. Living under a government ruled by Queen Daffodil is no way to live. Almost anything else has to be better than trying to live in those conditions."

"If they see you're unaccounted for, they're liable to search for you. Are you certain you haven't been followed?"

"I'm as certain as I can be. I don't expect to be noticed or missed, at least not for some time. Maybe by the next census, months from now."

"We have enough food to give you something to eat tonight, but you'll need to leave immediately after dawn. I don't want you here for very long. And don't ask a bunch of questions either. The less you know about us, the better it is for everyone. I don't want to exterminate you, but if you give us any trouble, I will."

"I certainly don't want to cause any trouble. If you can spare a bite to eat and possibly some grease for my chain, I'll be on my way this evening. I'm looking for a man named Carl. He has grease for my chain, but he may have been deloused."

"If you know someone who's been deloused, I wish you'd leave tonight, but I can't let you do that. You'll never survive the elements at night. The temperatures here drop to subarctic levels. Ever since the fallout from the bombs, the trees and vegetation that have survived can endure the freezing temperatures, but humans cannot. Mankind hasn't fully adapted yet. You will die. It will kill you. And we're not too far from one of the entrances to Queen Daffodil's underground lair."

Queen Daffodil lived in a subterranean palace hidden deep beneath the surface of the earth. Rumored to be hewed with platinum and gold 20 feet thick, diamonds and precious gems lined every walkway within the palace walls, except for the hallway to the dungeon's torture chambers. There was no glitter or glitz on those walls. The wise ones knew the rumors were true of The Queen and her evil doings. Some folks still didn't believe the rumors or tales of the wicked Queen; in their minds, there was no way The Queen could be behind the death and destruction across the planet. Rather, they regarded the stories of her evilness as false narratives, a conspiracy to distract everyone from an imaginary regime that had overthrown the government. After the worldwide bombings, coupled with the natural disasters that decimated the planet, its atmosphere, and water, Queen Daffodil was able to seize power and reign control over much of the globe. With her magic powers – the abilities to control in telepathy and energy manipulation – she had managed to rule for nearly 150 years.

"Queen Daffodil?" Ryder asked. "The evil sorcerer and ruler? *That* Queen Daffodil?"

"Yes, and I wouldn't take it lightly if you plan to survive out there. She is real and the things you've heard are true. She has psychic powers, and she lives in an underground kingdom not far from here."

Ryder considered Coyote's warning and found it easy enough to believe. It made sense as to why people's thoughts and actions against the corrupt government could be so easily discovered and controlled.

"If she lives so close, why doesn't she cause you any harm? Does she not know you're here? She's bound to know."

"Stop asking questions. I think she allows us to exist because we pose no threat to her. She doesn't care about a bunch of orphan kids, so if we keep to ourselves, she leaves us alone. At least for now, she has. We would never try to overthrow the government or steal from her. I think she knows that we have no means to harm her."

"Still, if you know where her secret lair is...that's valuable information. What if you were to sell that information to another budding government or regime? There's a lot of individuals who'd love to get their greedy paws on such information. I'm sure someone would pay dearly for information like that."

"Queen Daffodil has powers. Psychic powers. She has the ability to find us if she cares to. If we were to send any negative thoughts or energy her way, she could detect us. If she chooses, she can destroy us. She has a PRD, a psychic radar detector. It's a device that helps her detect where aggression is coming from. By using the PRD, she's able to pinpoint the exact location of those thoughts and actions. I, for one, know that her regime can never be trusted, but even if I were to give or sell that information to someone, even if they were wanting the information for good reasons with the goal of helping others and not just wanting to be another evil, greedy powermonger, even if I sold that information to someone good, there is *no* way we would *ever* get away with it. To believe otherwise is completely foolhardy. Queen Daffodil would torture and execute or enslave every last one of us. A fate worse than death is when she brainwashes people and turns them into slaves."

Coyote quit talking and shook his head from side to side. Ryder looked around at the procession of young children, moving with the zombie-like enthusiasm of lobotomized robot dolls, placing books and bits of broken furniture into two separate piles. Ryder wondered, *Who was brainwashing who?* Ryder didn't feel totally safe with Coyote, but realized he was correct in much of what he had to say. Still, Ryder speculated privately, *Who was brainwashing who? Why were these young children acting as if they were in a trance?*

Walking over to the piles of books and furniture, Ryder noticed a table leg carved with the intricate craftsmanship of a skilled woodworker. The table leg sticking up out of the pile was several centuries old. Every piece in the pile was an antique, hundreds of years old. Some pieces were probably a thousand years old or more, now broken into kindling. Examining the mounds of books, one in particular stood out and caught Ryder's attention. The firelight glistened off the gilded typeset of the title. Ryder picked up the book and read the title written in all capitals.

RESURRECTION
by LEO TOLSTOY

"Throw that in the fire," Coyote demanded. "None of this is worth keeping. We have to keep this fire blazing. Under no circumstance can this fire go out."

"Why? Aren't you worried about drawing attention to yourselves? What about the smoke billowing from the chimneys?"

"Since the bombings and the continued fallout from the volcanoes, the temperatures in this region, this spot in particular, can reach into the sub-zeros any time, day or night. But more important than that, the flames, the heat, and the smoke it creates keeps the Dire Wolves from beckoning our way. It's a repellent to them – the smell of the smoke, the fire, and the heat."

Ryder bent down to get a closer look at some of the other titles, most of which were written so long ago, they were unfamiliar. There was a book by man named Mark Twain and a book called *The Bible.* Ryder knew of that one. There was a book called *Mahābhārata* and another one on gardening. One book was labeled *The Koran*, another said *Auto Mechanics for Dummies.* Sitting on top of an unloaded wheelbarrow was a large, colorful book of artwork by a person named Salvador Dalí. Next to it was a little book with its pages sparsely worded by a woman named Emily Dickinson. Books by Charles Bukowski, John Steinbeck, Maya Angelou, and Flannery O'Conner lined the shelves. Ryder recognized the names of some modern writers, such as Zebraphon Humperdinck, Winona Waxahachie, Smithon Jones, Noah Billingsworth, Claudia Vonstoop, and Jim Neighbors. A few of these were the last books published, just before the first bombs fell and the Earth erupted into volcanic fire and ash.

"I didn't know anything like this still existed. Are you sure you want to destroy them?"

"They're all worthless. Throw them in the fire! We gotta stay warm. Now, stop asking so many questions."

Coyote peered intently at Ryder. Many thoughts raced through his head as he observed this strange person and their bike. Ryder opened one of the books, glancing at it and leafing through its pages.

"Where'd you get that bike from?" Coyote wanted to know.

Not waiting for an answer, he asked another question instead. "Can you understand those words on them pages?"

"Well, yes. Yes, I can. Some of these books are written in different languages, but the books written in English – yeah, I can read those."

"There's some things I might not be able to do, like reading, but there are lots of things I know about and things I know how to do. Most of these kids can't speak, but they communicate with sounds and thoughts. We've evolved beyond the need to speak to one another. Most of them can understand what I mean when I speak to them, but I'm one of the few in our cluster that has the gift of speech. We live here in this house and the surrounding area just fine. Like bugs under a stone…if we were forced to go somewhere else, I think we'd all die."

"Where are your parents? Are there any adults here?"

"We're orphans. Our parents and families died from war or famine or were killed by natural disasters and disease. Then, in a bizarre confluence of science and magic – for lack of any better explanation – we've been held in a suspended animation from a combination of radiation from the bombs and poisonous gas from the eruption of the volcanoes for over 150 years…as best I can calculate, give or take a half decade or so. We haven't aged since the disasters."

Ryder began to feel lightheaded, as though in a dream. Overwhelmed, it was difficult not to faint, based on the uncertainty of the realness of what Ryder saw and heard. Perhaps it was another hallucination, a figment of the distorted brain from the lack of proteins and vitamins. For a brief moment, wondering if any of this was real, Ryder reconsidered and decided that Coyote was real. Or, perhaps Coyote was the one hallucinating or imagining that he and these other psychic mute urchin companions were not stuck in time, not a century-and-a-half old, but merely starving teenagers. No matter the reality of either of their existences, the hair on the back of Ryder's neck started tingling. Feeling paranoid, Ryder decided it would be best to leave.

"I want to thank you for your hospitality, but I think I should continue with my journey."

"Don't be a fool! You'll never survive the cold. The night temperatures drop below zero every evening, no matter the time of year. And the Dire Wolves will sniff you out and rip you to shreds…and that's if you're lucky. If any of The Queen's guards catch you, the death will be much more painful and slow. They torture peasants for sport."

There was a long pause as Ryder considered Coyote's words.

"So, what's in them books? What does that book say?" Coyote asked. "Can you read it to me?"

"Yeah, I can read it to you. It says…" Ryder's voice trailed off.

Ryder happened to be holding a book entitled *The Grapes*

of Wrath by John Steinbeck. Ryder wasn't exactly sure, but reckoned it to be written over 500 years ago. He randomly opened the book, almost exactly in the middle, and read from the beginning of Chapter 19.

"This is by a guy named John Steinbeck. This is the beginning of Chapter 19," Ryder told him.

Ryder began to read. "'Once California belonged to Mexico and its land to Mexicans; and a horde of tattered feverish Americans poured in. And such was their hunger for land that they took the land, stole Sutter's land, Guerrero's land, took the grants and broke them up and growled and quarreled over them, those frantic hungry men; and they guarded with guns the land they had stolen. They put up houses and barns, they turned the earth and planted crops. And these things were possession, and possession was ownership.'"

Ryder stopped reading. Coyote was transfixed on the words. Ryder's ability to read amazed him, as well as the concepts and the meaning of the words coming from the pages.

Finally, Coyote spoke. "Well, I don't know who this John Steinbeck fella was, but not much has changed in hundreds and hundreds of years. People still steal, and the more powerful they are, the more they can steal and make whatever they want theirs. The only thing different is now there's nothing healthy left to steal. No farming or growing plants, nothing for food, no clean water, and no more riches. Wealth only exists for Queen Daffodil and a few others. There's no end to the greed and destruction on this planet or the pollution."

"That's not what I hear. I've heard there's an edge to this pollution."

"What?"

"I've heard rumors that there's an end to this perpetual grey toxic fog."

"You better not let anyone else hear you say that. Don't even think it! The Queen has ears in our thoughts. She knows. She can tell."

Coyote took in a deep breath and held it before speaking again. He said, "I'm sorry. You know what? I think you should leave. I think you should leave right now. I don't want to talk about this anymore. I don't even want to think about it. Stop thinking about it! Thought pollution can get you killed as easily as your actions will. I want you to leave. Get out! Now!"

The lanky boy delicately approached Coyote, and in a tongue only they understood, spoke to each other. The boy reminded Coyote of the temperatures and the Dire Wolves. Coyote changed his mind and allowed Ryder to sleep inside near the fire. Ryder was given a little bit of food to eat and was told to help stoke the fires throughout the evening. Ryder agreed and continued to throw broken pieces of antique furniture, some of which was handmade in the 1700s, onto the fire.

There were more books authored by Alex Haley, Emerson, Thoreau, and Hemingway, as well as those penned by more current celebrities, such as Brianna Newton-John and Noah Billingsworth. The autobiography by Noah

Billingsworth was a rather heavy and enormous book. When tossed onto the fire, it produced a loud thud and a rising array of smoldering cinders.

CHAPTER SIX

Crystal was all things real. She believed in the power of good and could sense a shift of the electricity in the atmosphere – a major change in the paradigm. She knew that the efforts her people had put into place were beginning to take shape. She could taste it on her tongue and in her nostrils. The air was becoming fresher, the skies were becoming clearer. Tonight's sunset was the clearest and most colorful of any sunset she could remember.

Ryder and Crystal were siblings, but they didn't know it. Their father fathered many children. Both of their moms were good people, raising them each to have decent morals and a soul with a conscience. Crystal's mom taught her to always trust in her psychic intuition and abilities.

Crystal grew up in a crystal mine 2,300 miles away from where Ryder was reared. They would never know each other as siblings; however, there was a cosmic wheel in motion that would have them crossing paths in a profound way one day. Crystal put her arm around her best friend and lover, Grace, her life and creative partner. Watching the sunset together and listening to the birdsong – a sound some thought had disappeared forever – the couple relished the moment. This was proof for both of them that this part of the planet was recovering. It proved that it was possible to spread the healing to all of Earth and its inhabitants.

CHAPTER SEVEN

The next morning, Ryder prepared for the journey. The ground was crispy and frozen with dew. One could see their own breath, even inside the mansion. Looking out the window at the frigid conditions, Ryder decided to return to the fire and wait another hour or two before taking off.

Hearing footsteps coming down the hall, Ryder stood up to see the lanky boy and the twins in braided pigtails, one of them carefully carrying a tray containing a hot bowl of porridge and a glass of crystal-clear water. This was an unexpected feast! Ryder had rarely had two meals in consecutive days. In fact, it had been ages since this kind of good fortune had occurred. Grateful for the nourishment from the night before and now a hot breakfast, Ryder gave thanks to the host and to the spirit world. Living on starvation pills and chalky purified mossy water was the extent of the most recent nourishment. *This* was actual food – porridge with a little bit of brown sugar and a sliver of butter.

"Oh my gosh. Where did you get this? It's delicious!" Ryder savored a small bite. The gangly boy and the twin girls made frantic gestures with their hands. They wanted Ryder to be quiet, so as to not alert anyone.

In a whisper, Ryder asked, "Where did you get this? How did you get this? Oh my God, is this sugar and butter?"

Ryder stirred it together and began scarfing down the hot food, blowing on each bite before engulfing the tasty morsels.

Between bites, Ryder, sounding urgent, asked, "Do you have any grease? I need grease for my chain."

The lanky boy and the pigtailed twins looked at Ryder like sympathetic aliens or children staring at a stray animal that they knew their parents would not let them keep.

"I gotta get grease for my chain, for my bike. Do you know where I can get grease for my chain?"

Ryder handed the empty bowl back to one of the girls. Ryder tried handing it to the lanky boy first, but he didn't respond. The boy was staring at Ryder, trying to figure out why this person was so taboo. They were warned vehemently and threatened with retaliation to stay away from Ryder.

One of the twins broke the silence by motioning for Ryder to hurry up and to remain quiet. Her hands and body language made everything perfectly clear: Ryder was to leave at once. With hands folded together, as if in prayer, Ryder bowed to the lanky boy and the twins in braided pigtails.

Outside, the air was more than brisk. Every breath was sharp, painful, and cut directly into the nostrils. The wind blew the frost through the trees. The sun already shone brightly, low on the horizon. Soon, the air and ground would warm. The crystallization of the morning dew would be no more.

Ryder rode with focused determination, penetrating through the forest, determined to avoid Queen Daffodil's hidden lair. Supposedly, her underground palace was to the east. Ryder knew the passage to the west was where the coast of the fabled Green Sea stretched, which led to a great city – a place where the last great vestige of the continent, and possibly the planet, existed. Mass communication no longer existed. It was a thing of the past. Hearsay and news were shared by word of mouth from strangers, from village to village. Sometimes, these sources were reliable, sometimes not. This was all that remained. And even that form of information was infrequent.

In no time, the temperature warmed considerably. The weather was perfect for riding. It was great weather for life, in general. And it was the first time ever that Ryder noticed how clean and fresh the air was. Birdsongs filled the air. Ryder couldn't remember ever hearing so many birds. Stopping for a moment to take it all in, Ryder paused and inhaled deeply, holding in the breath with eyes closed before letting it out in one powerful exhale. Wow, this feeling felt. . .healthy, exhilarating.

Ryder felt the rumors were true: This must be the place where Queen Daffodil lives because it must be the only decent space left on Earth with clean air. Maybe she used her magic to somehow keep the air clean? Or maybe the other rumors were true...that The People's People were hard at work fighting the good fight to rid the planet of evildoers, toxins, and pollution, and battling to replenish the Earth.

While riding through the forest, the comfortable weather and fresh air began to sour. Ryder could taste the sudden change. Sunny skies wrenched, filling the spaces between the trees. The sky turned to the color of a rotting corpse. Now, the air, acidic and bitter, was a grim reminder of gloom and death. Ryder's thoughts of turning back were dashed, seeing ominous clouds, swirling debris, and the darkening of nature in every direction. Unknown objects covering the path behind made turning around an impossible option.

With all of the surroundings suddenly unrecognizable and feeling fearful of death, Ryder started to sense that fate was out of control and accepted whatever outcome lay ahead. Calmness and fearlessness presided during this moment of acceptance. Ryder felt at peace. It seemed as though everything was moving in slow motion. Accepting one's own death, Ryder realized that no one needed to give up entirely and decided to not take it lying down.

Pointing the bike in what appeared to be the clearest path forward, Ryder took off through the forest in the opposite direction of the darkening nature erupting and roaring behind. Taking a deep breath, Ryder put every bit of weight and effort into pedaling, but the chain seized up immediately and the bike wouldn't budge.

Exhaling, Ryder felt it would be okay to die in this place. At least it wasn't at the hands of some cruel fate in the cold starkness of the heartless city. Everything was moving in slow motion. Debris and particles from decaying matter floated all around Ryder's face and hair. The wind began to blow harder from the impending force moving in from behind. Spitting and rubbing on the chain, Ryder managed to dislodge what was stuck within the sprockets. Ryder reset the chain and spun the wheel backwards, then caught the pedal by turning it forward, slipping the chain back on its gears. Staying calm, but knowing that speed was of the essence, Ryder mounted the bike and started to escape.

Feeling pressure, as if a freight train was barreling down upon them, the bike took off with a magical bolt of nature. The force of the wind lifted Ryder and the bike off the ground. Neither Ryder nor the bike were in control, but they flew through the air, delivered by the hand of fate, riding a cosmic gulfstream that carried them toward a bright light. It looked like the headlight of a northbound train or a giant lantern quickly growing in size. Ryder managed to stay on the bike that hovered just above the forest floor. The uneasy wind was cold. Rain and snow began falling, but the ground – the force from below – seemed to be expelling hot air that heated up the bike's handles and pedals. The light grew larger and brighter. Soon, it was all-encompassing, taking up everything in sight. It completely surrounded Ryder and the bicycle. Everything in the forest was exploding with disaster. A ball of light suddenly enveloped Ryder and the bicycle, shuttling them into a tube several miles below the Earth's surface. Inside the tube, Ryder vomited, nauseous from the pressurization involved with being transported several miles into the Earth's core. Eventually landing and disoriented from the fall, Ryder sat up and peered into the darkness.

"Sorry about that," a friendly voice called out from the dark.

Ryder, feeling a slight headache, but somewhat better after throwing up, looked around.

"Here, let me turn on some lights," the voice said.

A portly, slightly overweight man holding a plate of hot dogs flipped on a switch. Ryder began to see where they were. A stark, barren room, clinical with bright lights, similar to a hospital operating room…or possibly a really nice garage, minus any automobiles.

"Are you okay? Don't feel bad," the stranger said before continuing. "It's not your fault you got sick. That entry tube is supposed to adjust instantly to your heart rate and inner ear pressure, as well as your rapid eye movement. It should automatically adjust to any number of things, so the entry into this six-and-a-half-mile journey is smoother and won't make people sick and nauseous. You were traveling close to Mach One when you arrived. I'm not exactly sure why it's not functioning correctly. I invented the darn thing! It's supposed to make all these calculations and adjustments instantly, but there's still some bugs to work out."

The portly man chuckled and smiled. "I'm sorry, though. You should be okay in a few moments. Do you want a hot dog? As you can see, I like a lot of relish on mine."

Ryder couldn't believe what the man was saying. If it wasn't for feeling queasy and throwing up from motion sickness a few moments ago, one would think for certain that none of this was real. Maybe it wasn't real. If it was real, maybe this was what it was like to be dead.

The kind man interrupted Ryder's thoughts. "I know this has got to be strange. For God's sake, where are my manners? Let me get you some water."

He left for a moment and returned with a clear, hand-blown glass tumbler of filtered spring water with ice cubes.

He asked, "How are you feeling? I know this has got to be strange. Let me explain. You're safe here. Trust me, everything is okay. If you feel sick again, just let me know. I'll get you a bucket or show you to a restroom."

"No, thank you. I think I'm okay now," Ryder replied.

"Yeah, that entry tube needs some adjustments, but it's getting better. We're pretty close to figuring it out."

"Where did you get this?" Ryder had so many questions to be answered.

"What?"

"This!" Ryder held out the glass of cold water.

"Oh, that. We have a spring that runs through the rocks around us. It feeds right into our community down here. That glass you're drinking from is pretty cool, too. Maurice is really great at a lot of things, but he's a gifted glass artist. That glass is hand-blown," he responded while pointing with a half-eaten hot dog to the glass in Ryder's hand.

"How is this possible?" was all Ryder could say.

"It's a long story, but basically even before the destruction that decimated our planet, The People's People began setting up a network for survivors and talented thinkers ranging in a wide array of skills. Building an underground network below the Earth's surface, they found structures which were already here, probably built centuries ago. The founders weren't able to rescue as many people as they hoped, but many of our people have survived down here, as well as on the surface. However, due to the curious nature and volatile temperament of Queen Daffodil with her evil psychic abilities, our secrecy is of the upmost importance. Most of our people – The People's People up on the surface – don't even know we're down here. And they can't know in order to keep us safe. Some of them know of us, but there's only a handful of people on the surface that know exactly who we are. We're the only ones that can control the portal down here, so it's not a random accident or occurrence that you're here."

Ryder, no longer nauseous, was severely stunned by everything that just happened.

"Please, where are my manners?" the nice man asked before suggesting, "let's go inside."

Ryder looked around and noticed there were many doors along the seamless, curved white wall. A round room filled with doors. They were surrounded by doors. The room no longer felt like a hospital operating room, but a big garage. The cleanest garage you've ever seen. Ryder tried to count the number of doors, but consistently lost track. They seemed to be endless. It was impossible to tell exactly which door they had just come through or if they had fallen through the ceiling. Looking up, then down, then all around…

The man chuckled and said to Ryder, "Come on, you're bound to be tired and hungry. You can bring your bike inside if you'd like, but it'll be safe out here next to the door."

They walked through one of the doors, which opened into a posh living room adorned with elegant rugs, lamps, and artwork throughout. Thick oil paintings cased in large, intricate frames lined the walls. Life-sized statuesque figures carved out of stone were randomly placed around the room. The smell of hot dogs lingered in the air.

"We have all kinds of fresh foods. We have a garden, and we raise animals. Everything we produce, of course, we do here chemical-free. Even these hot dogs…or as healthy as a hot dog can be. But I can make you whatever you'd like. I'm sure you've been without regular food for some time."

"Those hot dogs smell amazing! I'll have one of those," Ryder replied.

"Okay, do you like mustard or ketchup? As you can see, I load mine up with relish."

"I don't care, I'm starving. However you're having them is fine."

Ryder stuffed down two hot dogs then started working on a third in the blink of an eye.

"I'm sorry. I've been yakking away and you're absolutely famished," the kind man stated.

Despite having a mouth full of hot dogs, Ryder couldn't resist asking questions in between bites. Questions that were barely comprehensible due to the sheer amount of food packed into Ryder's mouth.

"So, you said it was impossible to find this place and that it was no accident that I'm here," Ryder paused, gulped, and swallowed more of the hot dog before washing it down with cold water. Drinking cold spring water was as good as breathing in clean air. It was like drinking clean air.

Ryder pointedly asked, "Who are you and how is it possible that I'm here?"

"My name is Noah Billingsworth."

"The child star, celebrity, actor, and author? How is it possible that you're still alive? You must be several hundred years old."

"Yep, it's me. Do you need more water? Ice or no ice? You had ice, right?"

"You're Noah Billingsworth? Didn't you have a talk show, too?"

"Oh, God! Yes, I did. And it was terrible. Yeah, it's hard to believe the whole world was going to hell in a bucket, yet they kept re-running TV shows and talk shows hundreds of years old. If there was still the internet and electricity, they'd still be selling floor wax or subscriptions to something, just so they could keep airing that crap."

"I just saw your autobiography."

"Really, where? You've got to be shitting me."

"No, for real. I threw it on a fire last night."

"Well, that's where it belongs! It was too big to flush

down the toilet."

"I was taken in by a group of wild children living all alone in an estate on top of the mountain just east of here. Apparently, the weather is sub-zero in that region at night, so in an effort to stave off the Dire Wolves and the arctic temperatures, they keep a perpetual fire burning. In doing so, they're burning a library full of books."

"Oh, really?"

"Yes, and your autobiography was one of them."

"Was it any good?"

"I don't know. I didn't have time to read it. I was told to throw it on the fire, so I did."

"Good! I didn't even write the damn thing. I thought the entire book was stupid, but my publicist and office thought it was brilliant. 'Ride the wave, it'll save your career…blah blah blah'. But here's what I'm good at." Noah waved his hand in the air, the one holding a hot dog.

Both of them stood in silence eating hot dogs, a plate in one hand and a hot dog in the other.

Ryder finally broke the silence, "This? This is what you're good at? Eating hot dogs in a fancy apartment several miles below the Earth's surface?"

"No. Well, yes…but no. I'm a scientist. I designed all this. I'm an echo-specialist, an astrophysicist, and a biologist. I'm an expert in space and earth science. I'm an environmentalist and an inventor who has been involved with The People's People movement since its inception. I have developed telepathic communication skills and machines that enhance that sort of activity. My colleagues and I have been thoroughly studying advanced psychic teleportation communication techniques so we can transmit and receive transmissions with the space colonies on Mars. Even without the use of normal electricity. And we've been studying energy and the reality of transmitting energy and thoughts, similar to sound waves. That's where you come in."

"Okay, I can buy into a lot of different things. And I don't doubt cosmic mind control stuff; I do believe unexplained ESP-type of things can happen. I think that's entirely possible, but I don't know how I come into any of this. One thing I do know, though, it was weird as shit to be engulfed by a dark cloud one minute and now I'm here and you're telling me all this weird stuff. So why? Why me? Why am I here? Is this what it's like to be dead?" Ryder inquired.

Billingsworth chuckled and looked over his spectacles while rhetorically answering Ryder with, "Why are any of us here?"

Noah Billingsworth is not a tall man, not grossly overweight, but rounded in places. When he peers at someone over his glasses, he has an intuitive nature to read them instantly. He's able to shed cosmic grandfatherly psychedelic wisdom, as if saying with a glance over his spectacles, 'I have you figured out, even if you don't have yourself figured out'. Noah Billingsworth did have people pegged as soon as, or even before, a person stepped foot into a room. He wasn't the silly, charismatic buffoon that he played on TV. No, he was much smarter than that. Brilliant, beyond genius-level smart.

He started off in the television industry, starring in commercials as a child actor. He had an inquisitive mind and invented cosmic technology far beyond the comprehension of most adults before he reached puberty. Television made his family a fortune, affording him the luxury to work on his mind's inventions and build an underground lair fit to transmit and receive messages to other planets in an effort to help save Earth.

CHAPTER EIGHT

After several plates of hot dogs and potato chips, Noah Billingsworth shared explicit details with Ryder about his understanding and development of technologies, real and tangible, as well as other forms of psychic science, the mental powers and energy of thoughts, and the ability to control things with one's mind. Not thought control like hypnosis, but a form of thought control that involved tapping into the energies of the mind and all the possibilities that the human brain might possess. Things that we are just now tapping into in the 31st century.

"Okay, you've filled me in on as much as I can handle or comprehend. So far, this cosmic experiment or concept of yours seems to be working. I haven't seen the full extent of your dwellings yet, but what I *have* seen is very impressive. You transported me over six miles into the Earth, into this place, and the hot dogs are delicious, so you definitely have your shit together. But how in the hell do I fit in?"

"If you would please follow me," Noah directed. "By the way, are you full for now? I have banana pudding and there's still some chocolate cake if you want some. It's really good. You should have some later if you like sweets. Would you like a beer?"

Ryder turned down the offer of cake or beer and said, "Maybe later."

Billingsworth grabbed a beer for himself then opened the door to a small laboratory that appeared to serve more as an office than a lab. Two overstuffed leather couches, one of which had a pillow and blanket ruffled up on it, sat end to end of each other in a row facing the wall. Covering the walls were large chalkboards containing scribbles of theories and equations that had been erased, re-erased, and then re-scribbled. There were other chalkboards, movable ones on wheels, that also had theories and equations written out in meticulous detail.

Billingsworth turned to Ryder and said, "Hold my beer." He walked over to one of the three chalkboards on wheels and spun it around for Ryder to see. Written in white chalk were these words followed by a drawing:

CHAPTER EIGHT

I am on a linear track.
You are a wavelength.
Our paths will only cross at certain junctures.

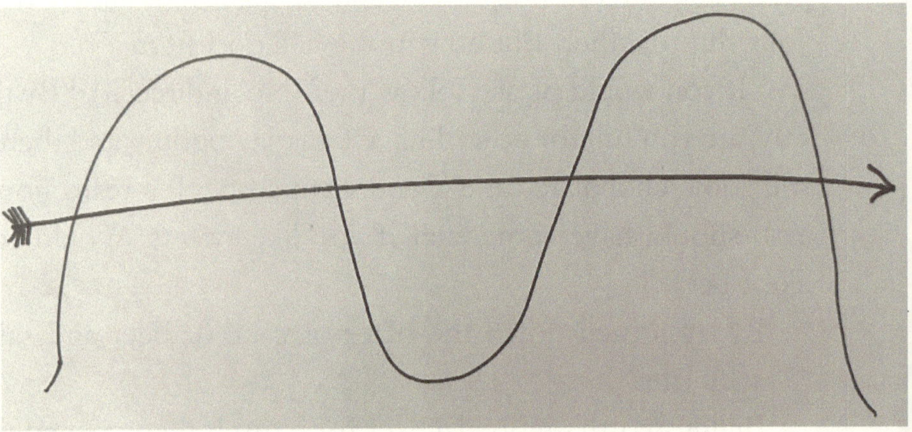

"Well, that's fucking weird."

"Tell me about it! I keep having these words pop into my head. I had a dream with them. No, wait…maybe I had the dream first. Maybe I had a dream and didn't realize it. I kept having these words pop into my head subconsciously over and over again throughout the day. At night, I dreamt about those words and that drawing written on a chalkboard. And ever since then, that image has been etched into my brain," Noah stated while pointing to the image on the chalkboard.

He paused before asking, "Does it mean anything to you?"

"Well, it doesn't mean anything to me, per se, but this is the third time it has shown up to me either in written form or verbally. The first time was by a mysterious nymph who appeared out of the steam and fog in the city where I'm from. She spoke with the most delicate angelic voice I've ever heard. If it were possible for the sound of words to be soft, delicate whispers of petals from a flower, her words would've been just that. The girl with the soft rose petal whispers, those were her words. Then this lanky boy outside the mansion, the estate full of urchins, walked up to me and handed me a scroll with those words written out and that same drawing etched on your chalkboard. The same thing that the girl with the soft rose petal whispers told me."

"But how did I dream this?" Noah Billingsworth asked. "It makes me think that a cosmic higher power, one that even I don't understand, is at play."

CHAPTER NINE

Crystal and Grace started their day by receiving good news then relaying it to the others. Their hopes and efforts were beginning to pay off. Many miles away from The Crystal City, the army of The People's People had withstood a severe attack, forcing back the advancing troops and saving their hidden capital from the dangers of being discovered. With the retreat and withdrawal of Queen Daffodil's corrupt army, it gave opportunity for The People's efforts to take hold. The pollution and poisonous toxins surrounding her evil forces were still an issue, lingering in the environment long after they left the region…but they were showing signs of diminishing. It had taken some time, but the efforts to restore the planet were beginning to take hold.

Many of the younger rebels had never seen blue skies. Birds had almost become extinct. Remarkably, a lone sparrow – then another, and another – landed on the ground just a few feet from where the two lovers stood. It was a sign of good things to come, but now was not the time to rest on their accomplishments. More efforts were needed in order for the positive changes to continue. Both women, central figures and leaders of The People's People movement, were looked upon for the next course of action. Those whose families survived the torment and torture over the centuries prior leading to this moment knew to take nothing for granted. Despite having the evildoers on the run, most people knew not to let their guard down. In spite of their caution, everyone couldn't help feeling elated.

With the recent turn of events, the village could breathe a collective sigh of relief. People were beginning to believe that good would triumph over evil. They *would* survive. They *would* pull through. Little did they know their days until the planet's demise could be numbered. They didn't realize that in spite of the positive turn of events and the hopeful signs that the planet could rebound and that mankind could survive, their existence was actually about to evaporate, gone forever in the blink of an eye, leaving no trace of ever existing unless critical measures were to happen. The brink of annihilation, evaporation of everything on the planet would most likely occur in less than 40 days and 40 nights. It was critical. Certain factions needed to be brought together for the greater good of mankind.

CHAPTER TEN

"Dreams are weird," Ryder said.

"I have no idea how you could dream something like that and then end up writing it on a chalkboard. I have no idea why a group of filthy urchins would have the same words written on a scroll, or why a mysterious nymph whispered this to me before disappearing into the shadows of the city one evening."

"Well, there's a cosmic messenger at play," Noah Billingsworth replied matter-of-factly. "Here's something I do know. People – you, me, everyone – we all have different energy. Not a big surprise there. But different energy, how we vibrate, all of the individual molecules that make us who we are, all of that stuff, our individual stuff, our molecules, our vibrations, our energy…it's all a unique cosmic fingerprint that's unique to us. Each one of us has our own chemical element, like in the periodic tables. And like the elements in the periodic table, we all have – each and every one of us – our own symbol and number that's unique to us. This is our own cosmic fingerprint. It's similar, but different than our DNA. Just like sulfur's chemical element symbol is S and its atomic number is 16, and a substance like vinegar, because it has acetic acid, is CH3 COOH, and baking soda is NaHCO3, and so on, and so forth…people have their own chemical element number, too. Some are completely individual and even rarer than an O+ blood type. You don't know her yet, but Crystal, the person, has a chemical element number that's unlike anyone else's on Earth. The only people with two of the similar elements in their cosmic periodic table number are you and another person named Nora. Nora is the child of a shaman named Elizer. We know this from the information that we've collected on most every living soul on Earth. Crystal is the key element to make our thought energy waveforms reach Mars. The efforts we've accomplished in reversing the ecological damage to our planet will not succeed without a special substance unique to Mars. With this substance, we can reverse the damage to the atmosphere of the planet, ultimately returning it to a healthy balance of oxygen and nitrogen, which all livings things on the planet need to survive."

"Okay, I'm not sure if I completely understand," Ryder said reluctantly.

Billingsworth thought for a moment and replied, "Okay, here's another example. When you add vinegar to baking soda, you get a chemical reaction that causes the energy to change, and the two elements will bubble, foam, and erupt. The same is true with humans, but on a much deeper level. Imagine a big cosmic machine where each cog in this cosmic contraption has its own unique identifier. Copper is Cu on the periodic table, titanium is TI, and so on. We have discovered that if we find the magic, unique periodic human combination of people and use their individual and unique brain powers to come together in a harmonious, synchronized endeavor, we can transverse the normal confines of space and time, thus allowing us, for instance, to time travel. Not in a linear way, like going back to the past or forward to the future, but in a right-now way, in the present moment. If we pull this off, and we're very close to having all the pieces of the cosmic mental cogs that we need, we can instantly transverse time and space, and instantly be on another part of the continent, or Earth, or even the moon, or Mars. Theoretically, we'll be able to get back to one of the colonies on Mars…provided they haven't also been overthrown or crumbled in the fallout similar to what happened to our planet, knocking us back in time to a life of no electrical power, which you have now experienced for the past 150 years. We've figured out through our extensive research and the experiments that I've conducted that if we combine specific combinations of certain people with mental telepathy potentials, or MTP, put together into one force, just like the combinations of baking soda and vinegar, we can create a reaction that will not only transmit messages, thoughts, etcetera, but solid objects. People, and hopefully, entire civilizations, moved in an instant! Just before our power systems collapsed after the eruptions at Yellowstone, the space station and the colonies on Mars still heavily relied on Earth for transmissions in the receiving of telecommunications. Even if the space stations and the colonies on Mars still have the capabilities to send electronic messages, we wouldn't be able to receive the transmissions without a working power grid. We need to harness these powers using Crystal's mind and her thought powers in order to transmit a message to Mars. She has a unique chemical element; her cosmic fingerprint is like no other."

"Well, I still don't see how I fit into all of this," Ryder sighed. "Am I really part of the mental chemical equation to join mental forces to transmit a message?"

"Yes, you are, but more important than that, we need you to get this information through to Crystal and Grace and their team of scientists and environmentalists. Even though we're beginning to successfully communicate this way, in order for it to work, the people on the receiving end of the message must be clued into the technology. If they don't know to turn on their device, how can they receive a message? Unless they know where to tune in or how to tune in, they won't get the message. And here's where you come in: we need you to be our human carrier pigeon. You have to get a message through to this woman named Crystal who's leading The People's People efforts in reclaiming the water and air from the government. Even though on top of the planet's surface, they've been without a worldwide power grid for over a century and a half. Down here, we've created our own electricity to run everything from our creature comforts to our experiments. We grow our own food in greenhouses similar to what they've developed on the space stations and on the colonies of Mars. Living here inside Earth isn't as great as living outside on Earth…when there was fresh air, food, and water. Hopefully that's going to change with the leadership of people like Crystal and Grace," Billingsworth explained.

He continued, "We're down here doing our part, too. And when Sirius reaches its highest apex this season in just over an Earth month and 10 days, that's when we need every mind in this particular equation to be focused as one. The biggest hurdle we face now is that Crystal doesn't have this information. But, with all of us directing our thoughts in unison with her, even if we aren't in the same location, we can make this work if the right mixture of people combine their mental energy and focus on the same intention at the same time."

Billingsworth took a bite of chocolate cake and went on to say, "Crystal is the central component of this cosmic compound in the equation. It won't work without her being the point of our compass."

"How so?" Ryder asked.

"She's not named Crystal by accident. It's divine intervention. She was born in a crystal mine full of crystals, just like the ones we use to power our lasers and computers. These crystals, these very special crystals that come out of the earth where she was born and raised, act as transmitters for cosmic energy – things that are real and tangible, as well as the unexplained happenings that they produce into the ether. Crystal is the most powerful human transmitter on the planet. And she doesn't even know it."

"How do you know this?"

"The same way we knew to capture you to help us connect the cosmic cogs. We just do. It's been written, so to speak, on tea leaves before all existence existed. It's been meditated on, and the visions have been interpreted. We have deduced our conclusions through a series of intuitions, science, and the art of throwing monkey bones and sticks into the air and reading into what they tell us. We use science and philosophy, voodoo, witchcraft, prayer, and some really badass computers. Oh yeah, that's right. We probably have the only functioning computers left on Earth, including the original ancient IBM computer that runs off punch cards. It takes up the space of an entire house. I'll show it to you if you like. But I digress…Crystal has a unique chemical equation, and we need her to be tuned in so we can get a cosmic message to the space colonies on Mars. I don't want to freak you out, but if this doesn't work, the planet is doomed. We need you to be a human carrier pigeon. We need you to get a message through to Crystal with all the exact details and coordinates."

Ryder paused momentarily to let the information sink in before responding. "Okay, I'm only getting a little freaked out. But why me? Why must I be the one?"

"Because, like I was telling you earlier, you and Crystal

share similar and very unique properties in your chemical equations, creating a higher probability for this to be successful. You must be the one to deliver the message. It's in the cards. It's your destiny. There's a law of attraction here. Like a magical, magnetic gravitational force, our cosmic analysis tells us that this is so. Fate brought you to us. We tried our best to will it into being; and the hand of fate is the one who has touched us and brought us to this moment."

"Okay. Well, I guess I better get going. I need supplies and grease for my chain. It seized up on me when I was escaping the storm, the one that blew me into your portal."

Billingsworth reassured Ryder. "Don't worry. We'll get you grease for your chain. And even though it's imperative to reach Crystal in a timely manner, we actually have to wait until the timing is right and everything is in alignment. Like a maze within a wheel, with each pathway moving in contra motion of one another, each one at different tempos, there will be a moment in time when all of the openings will line up and you can travel through. That's when the chances of you succeeding are greatest. It's imperative for you to reach the village where Crystal and Grace live. They live at the foot of the crystal mine, just on the edge of the continent overlooking the West Coast."

"How will you know when the time is right for me to leave?" Ryder asked.

"We're following the stars and charting the paths of the zodiac, kind of like the weather. We wait and try to forecast when the journey will be safest to begin. In the meantime, let me show you around."

Noah Billingsworth's underground lair was built in a random configuration of long hallways and stairs leading to magnificent rooms that were attached to more hallways and stairs and corridors leading to other rooms designed in various shapes and sizes, splintering in all directions, all used for many different purposes. Some of the hallways and stairs were like those of ornate palaces. Beautiful carpets and rugs covered the floors. Hallways were lined with detailed glass tiles in brilliant colors, shiny brass handrails, and mirrored ceilings. A few passages were small tubular portals, resembling those on a submarine: dank and dimly lit, rounded concrete tunnels with exposed ductwork and cables. There were greenhouses, magnificent structures, like something one would expect to see at the space station. A centuries-old billiards room occupied one area, with its dark crimson leather couches and chairs, and regulation-sized billiards and snooker tables. There was a bar stocked with tequila, brandy, scotch, and whiskey stored in barrels hundreds of years old. A walk-in humidor was loaded with rich, earthy, aromatic hand-rolled cigars from the finest tobacco grown anywhere. There was a sauna, steam bath, and an Olympic-sized swimming pool. The kitchen and dining room were immaculate and grander than anything Ryder thought imaginable. Most of their meals, all of them except one, were served at a small round wooden table that sat by the windows in the corner of a large kitchen. Even though they were miles underground, looking through the windows, it appeared as though they were looking out onto a beautiful pastoral scene with rolling grassy knolls, spotted with cows and sheep grazing within a white plank fence. There was a dairy barn in the background with a tall round silo for storing grain. The sun shone at the appropriate time of day, as if it was on Earth. In the evenings, one could see the stars or walk out onto the porch and gaze out into a holographic sky that moved and rotated like Earth on its axis.

The kitchen was one of the most comfortable rooms in the house. That's where they spent a good deal of their time in conversation. This room was a favorite of Ryder's and Noah's. Another room was also a favorite of theirs: Noah called it his "study". Not to be confused with the den, which was also a very cozy room appointed with old, worn-in furniture and a fireplace.

The study was a favorite room to pass the time of day or night because Noah Billingsworth had an ancient contraption known as a record player. He possessed a large collection of music that was stored on and played off round vinyl discs that Billingsworth called 'LPs,' which included a style he referred to as 'jazz' and another completely different form, 'classical'. These were two styles of music, totally divergent and contrasting from one another in every way, neither of which Ryder had ever heard before. Ryder learned that with classical music, the musicians were playing the music note for note as it was written on the page, but with the jazz music, certain parts or themes were written then the musicians would improvise their solos over the chord changes of the song. Billingsworth explained to Ryder that with classical music, some composers, like Bach, for example, were from the 1600s and 1700s, while other composers, such as Beethoven, were from the 1700s and 1800s. Noah played Ryder a piece from 1913 called "The Rite of Spring" by Igor Stravinsky.

"When it was first performed, it was so radical and avant-garde, the crowd erupted into a frenzy. The audience became so riled up and out of hand, they couldn't continue with the performance. It caused such a disturbance that parts of the theater were torn apart, and a riot broke out. 'The Rite of Spring' became 'The Riot of Spring,'" Billingsworth joked.

He paused, expecting a chuckle, but when Ryder didn't respond, he continued. "It wasn't performed again for several years, and it wasn't until much later that it was regarded as a masterpiece and one of the greatest works of the 20th century."

Ryder had never heard of any of the music Noah Billingsworth played. Within the genre of jazz, Noah loved saxophone players. His favorite was Wayne Shorter, but he also played a lot of music featuring Dexter Gordon, Sonny Rollins, and John Coltrane. The bassist and composer Charles Mingus and trumpeter Miles Davis were two other jazz artists who Noah would go on and on about. Noah Billingsworth enjoyed the piano playing of McCoy Tyner and Red Garland. He also played records by Ray Barretto and Mongo Santamaria. With his classical collection, he listened to everything from Beethoven to Bartok, Chopin, Mendelssohn, Tchaikovsky, Schubert, Mozart, and Brahms.

Ryder was fascinated with the entire process that went into listening to each record. The smell of the old paper from the cover and the inner sleeve. Transfixed, Ryder watched Noah carefully remove the vinyl records from the sleeve, being mindful to only touch the record by the edges with his fingers. He never touched the album with his fingertips. He said this was to keep the grease from his skin off the vinyl. He then carefully chose which side to play and placed it on the turntable before lowering the needle onto the grooves in the record. He carefully cleaned any minute particles with a cleaner as the record spun around on the turntable. The sound system was completely captivating, and they slipped into a meditative hypnosis, listening intently whenever the music was playing. Sometimes, they made comments, but they usually sat quietly and without interruptions during the listening experience. Noah frequently pointed out certain aspects of the music or the history behind the piece of music that was playing, but usually they sat focused, mesmerized by the magical sounds coming out of a contraption hundreds of years old.

Another ancient device that brought them hours of entertainment was an original 8mm film projector. Noah explained how everything involved with the film worked. He drew out diagrams on one of the large chalkboards that illustrated the functions of how everything worked – from the camera and the projector to how the film was developed. Billingsworth had a cardboard box full of rolls of random home movies, mostly from the 1960s and 70s. He didn't know anyone in any of the three-minute films. The films had no sound, so after repetitive viewings, the silent strangers had become familiar friends. There were birthday parties and backyard cookouts, various people smiling and waving to the camera. The film rolls boasted a wedding, high school or college graduations, family vacations (one to the Grand Canyon, in particular), homecoming parades, and bar mitzvahs. Several were from Christmas mornings, and one was from a soapbox derby.

Even though it was a different time several hundred years ago, it made each of them nostalgic and homesick for a life they didn't know…but homesick, just the same. Homesickness transverses all times and languages. It made them both miss something neither of them ever had. It was a reminder of home and of a strange normalcy they had been denied.

Besides being one of the most brilliant minds in all things science, Noah Billingsworth was also a master historian and an expert in almost every field: art, music, alchemy, and any form of earth and space science. He wasn't alone in the development of the use of the quantum powers of the brain and the mental psyche, but he was the primary leader in the discovery of this technology. Whereas hundreds of years before it was believed that we only used about 10 to 12 percent of the brain's potential, Noah Billingsworth was close to breaking through to enabling all people to use 80 percent.

CHAPTER ELEVEN

As impressive as the entire underground lair was, the laboratory, without a doubt, was the most impressive room of them all. It was radically different from anything that had ever existed, and to this day (about 6,000 years later), it stands as a feat unequaled to anything devised by mankind or any other intelligent being within the universe.

"This is where our team harnesses thought energy, which we can turn into power. We can use it as electricity or turn it into ultrasonic sound waves that travel 40,000 times faster than the speed of light."

Billingsworth walked over and put his hand on a semicircular crystal about as big as a Volkswagen Beetle and proudly explained, "This baby here is what we're using to break down the molecules of solid objects, people included. We're able to transmit them in just under 37 times the speed of light. The only problem with our attempts to transport actual objects is the random interference of gamma rays. Gamma rays rarely, yet occasionally, have interfered with the experiments. Random occurrences that seem to have come from nowhere with no warning, making it impossible to detect them in advance."

Noah Billingsworth was a child star in the late-1970s through the 1980s. He had moderate success as an adult with several talk shows and a variety show, none of which lasted more than a season; one of the talk shows was canceled less than halfway through the first season. Even though he was thought to be dead for over five and a half centuries, his shows had become wildly popular and somewhat of a cult classic with a following lasting long after his presumed death. Billingsworth and his team of scientists and experts had been kept alive because of a science he developed, along with the help of a few other biochemists, molecular engineers, and naturopathic psychic energy healers, within a suspended animation chamber. The technology for him to live back on the Earth's surface was untested and unproven, and it was unknown whether he could survive after being kept alive underground for many centuries. But there was a team of scientists and specialists working to devise a method so that one day, that would be possible.

The suspended animation chamber was comprised of

cryogenics and molecular transfusion; essentially, the exchange of dead or dying atoms and molecules for regenerated copies of the existing person or object. Carbon copies were made by a device that took virtual X-rays of the atoms, their form, and equation, and then replicated them instantly inside the person or object before transmitting it to a new location. The transmission was the most difficult part of the procedure – and one of the main reasons Noah Billingsworth lived underground for the past five-and-a-half centuries. It's actually only centuries, at least as we know it on Earth and in our galaxy. Time is irrelevant to mankind, just as it was timeless in Noah Billingsworth's suspended animation chamber. Hours, days, weeks, centuries were mere blips in time down in Noah's sprawling universe.

Noah Billingsworth's genius and brilliant mind went unnoticed as a child. Thought to be bizarre or weird, his parents, teachers, and clergy equated it to being mentally challenged or somewhere on the spectrum. Misunderstood and shunned by his peers, it wasn't until he was an adult when he met two cohorts who understood him and propelled his theories and hypothesis into reality.

They were two brothers, named Joshua and Jeremiah Moynihan. The Moynihans were short and stout individuals. Both had facial hair covering their chins, but none on their lips, much like that of the Quakers. They were rarely seen, but lived inside the underground lair, along with Billingsworth and a team of scholars and scientists, most of whom were several centuries old (at least by Earth standards).

The Moynihans were both geniuses. Together, they formulated and manufactured the science that enabled the suspended animation chamber to exist. They were also key to the development and discovery in determining the theories behind individuals' body chemistry. They created the science behind the ability to combine the cosmic equation of two individuals or a group of individuals and generate a totally new and unique cosmic equation, thereby forming a compound of specialized focused energy with the intention of transmitting messages psychically from one planet to another.

Charismatic and debonair, the brothers were boisterous and jovial. They lit up the room anytime they broke away from their experiments, joking and clowning around with the other staff or residents in the clandestine community. They were always the life of the party. Joshua and Jeremiah were in charge of other departments inside the chambers as well. Rarely seen, they did, however, accompany Ryder and Billingsworth on a few late-night dinners and discussions. The discussions were not only on the current situation to save Earth from devastation and destruction, but on art and literature, music and film, politics and social decorum. Both Joshua and Jeremiah were excellent storytellers, and they could also tell a good joke. Most of their stories were full of humorous tales of the shenanigans that happened while growing up in a large Catholic family…and the pranks and whippings that entailed. They told stories in unison, often finishing each other's sentences.

Ryder sensed that there were other workers or employees

in this underground existence, but didn't really see anyone except for Billingsworth, the Moynihans, and the Gutridges, the cooks in Noah's underground lair.

One night, Noah and Ryder were hanging out and listening to Charles Mingus on the phonographic stereo when Ryder asked, "What happens if it doesn't work? What happens if it fails? Think of all the things that could go wrong."

"Think of all the things that could go right!" Noah said. "There was a great philosopher and poet from many centuries ago named Rumi who said, 'Never lose hope, my dear heart, miracles dwell in the invisible.'"

He paused then continued speaking. "I read a lot of texts and literature from throughout the ages, over many centuries. It keeps me from going insane. It's one of the benefits of living down here in a timeless vacuum – I have all the time in the world to read and ponder. One day, when we do figure out a way that I can materialize back into the world, I'll have read and absorbed many thousands of books that I've chosen to read. Anything that's ever been written over the course of time, I have time to read it. There's no way a person could ever do that living within the restraints of a linear timeline. Here's another good thing I read the other day…it pertains to what you just said about worrying about the bleakness of the circumstances that the planet is in. It's a quote by a man named Desmond Tutu. He also lived many centuries ago. He said, 'Hope is being able to see that there is light despite all the darkness.'"

"Who was Desmond Tutu?" Ryder asked.

"Desmond Tutu was an Anglican cleric and theologian from South Africa. He was known for his works as an anti-apartheid and human rights activist over 500 years ago," Noah elaborated. "The point is, you gotta have faith, and you gotta hope and trust in each other. You have to hope and trust and believe that we *will* survive. We *will* get by. You *will* succeed."

"Let's do this. Why aren't we acting right now? Time is wasting!"

"Time is not the same here. Time is ill-relevant. By the time you re-enter that realm, nary a nanosecond will have expired. We have to wait until the exact, perfect moment to arrive. Similar to watching the weather map on an ever-evolving radar screen, Moynihan and his brother are overseeing a team of experts that's calculating all forms of energy fields to determine precisely when you should re-enter your former existence. Determining these exact coordinates will ensure us the greatest odds for success."

"I hope I'll be ready. I hope I can handle it," Ryder replied.

"Don't fill yourself full of doubt. When the opportunity comes knocking, you need to have room to let it in. Believe in yourself and those around you, and you'll be ready."

Billingsworth went on to explain. "Everything in the universe is made of light vibrating at different frequencies. Humans, even the table in front of you, vibrate at a slower rate; so, we appear solid, but our essence is pure light. We're working on the technology to transform our very vibrations first to liquid then to light. Once we accomplish this, we can transcend time and space…and eventually travel through time. Not time travel, like into the past or the future, but in the here and now. We could travel from one location to another in an instant. Are you hungry? Mrs. Gutridge should be ready to serve us dinner. I believe that tonight is Beef Wellington, with roasted potatoes, asparagus, and cream of pea soup for a starter. I'm not certain if dessert will be profiteroles or hazelnut meringue, but either way, we're in for a treat."

CHAPTER TWELVE

Crystal and Grace awoke cheerfully. Both ladies were feeling good about the recent progress made by The People's People. The air was becoming cleaner and clearer every week. Natural water sources were starting to flow, and smaller tributaries, streams, and rivers were beginning to clear up. Treetops thrived with healthy vegetation and a variety of birds. Other creatures, such as insects, reptiles, mammals, fish, and plants of many forms were showing signs of recovery. Spirits in The Crystal City and the surrounding camps were high, and a joyful buzz was all about. The good mood was cut short when a messenger in distress rode into camp on horseback bringing some serious news.

Queen Daffodil had dispatched 350 soldiers, as well as armored trucks, bulldozers, and assault vehicles armed with machine guns and 20mm cannons. The brigade was marching through The Blue Forest, bulldozing and destroying everything in its path. The tiny hamlet of Ector was destroyed and torched to the ground upon its discovery. Anyone – man, woman, or child – found alive after the bombs and inferno was tortured and suffered a slow death. It was said that Queen Daffodil herself was out in the field, leading the charge and coordinating the attacks and torture. She was carted around in a chariot made of precious metals and gems, gilded with gold, emeralds, and pearls. The handles were made from extinct animal tusks and the cushions were lined with rare furs and human skin. The bones and teeth from the children of her adversaries adorned her wrist and neck.

After a victory, the sadistic, conquering Queen Daffodil could be seen drinking the blood of her victims from a platinum chalice. "The younger the blood, the sweeter the victory," she often stated.

Queen Daffodil was a rather large creature. To cover her bulbous shape, she dressed in a bright yellow gown accented by a long, trumpeted crown that rose two feet above her head. Whenever other people's suffering pleased her, her laughter was like a fever dream, barking out a brass staccato 'Ha ha ha ha' in a nightmarish howl. Evil graveled in her throat. Bloodstained teeth, darkening the moonlight and turning daylight into shadows. Her presence seeped toxins into all living things. Despair and a bloodcurdling paralysis spread within every man and beast any time she drew near.

Upon hearing the news, Crystal and Grace initiated protocol, alarming the workers and families in the city and camps to take shelter. The People's People were set into action. Code Red alerted the villagers to hide from Queen Daffodil's forces and to misdirect them in their attempts to locate the village camps surrounding The Crystal City. Each person had a duty to fulfill and was carefully trained to follow a step-by-step process to camouflage and avert the detection apparatus that The Queen and her henchmen deployed in their attempts to locate The People's camp. Bungalows, cliff dwellings, hutches, cabins, teepees, and tents were suddenly hidden with a complex and specific form of cloaking camouflage that masked detection by the naked eye, as well as from any form of psychic radar or heat-seeking devices.

The messenger wasn't sure what direction the troops were headed, but she knew for certain they were at least 100 miles away. The very rugged terrain that stretched between them and The Queen's army was their only hope. This bought The People's People more time to prepare their defenses in case Queen Daffodil and her evil minions were to stumble upon them.

CHAPTER THIRTEEN

Noah Billingsworth and Ryder were in the den listening to jazz records after a delicious meal prepared for them by Mrs. Gutridge and her skinny husband, Gus. Gus Gutridge was merely her helper. Mrs. Gutridge, a skilled chef, always prepared meals with the freshest ingredients. She was a plump woman with rosy cheeks and the appearance that she enjoyed her own cooking. Gus was a tall, rail-thin man who looked like he hadn't had a decent meal in weeks. With deep lines running through emaciated cheekbones, Gus Gutridge looked as though he were a bum living on Skid Row.

Noah and Ryder were enjoying port by the fire as

Billingsworth explained the music spinning on the turntable. He said, "I love this record. It's called *In A Silent Way* by Miles Davis. This record is from 1969."

"Wow, that's over 500 years ago."

"The late-1960s period of Miles Davis is one of my favorites. It's probably the most innovative period of jazz from that time period. All of it leading up to the seminal work of art, a recording called *Bitches Brew* from 1970."

"Noah, I've got to be honest. I'm not sure if I can do what you need of me," Ryder admitted.

"It's very important we get this message through. The mathematical coordinates will be written out with very specific instructions for you and Crystal, explaining how to concentrate and focus as a unified telepathic beam that will be sent to the humans on the colonies of Mars. We're convinced that if we can align both our thoughts and focus at the precise astronomical moment, we can override a communication source at the Cuban headquarters on Mars."

"Why the Cuban base on Mars? Why not the American colony on Mars?"

"Because indicators tell us that the US colony on Mars has been shut down by some sort of disturbance. Possibly an inside job."

"I don't know if I have the strength or mental fortitude to carry this out. It's such an important obligation. I never imagined this would be my calling," Ryder said.

"The universe has always been playing out in you," Noah said. "You are infinite."

"I've often wished for a greater purpose, something more

than just the regular fight or flight to survive. Maybe this *is* my purpose? With the oppression we live in constantly, the fear and destruction brought on by Queen Daffodil and her corrupt government, I've always felt small, insignificant, and fearful. I've lived my entire life looking over my shoulder, trapped by my own devices or those bestowed upon me by the existence I was born into. How do I reckon with that and have faith that I can carry out this task you ask of me?"

"Over 100 years before Miles Davis and the invention of American jazz, there was a great Native American chief named Black Elk, who once said, 'Freedom comes within the souls of men when they realize their oneness with the universe.'"

After a long pause, Noah repeated something he mentioned earlier. "You are infinite, the whole universe is being played out in you. We are multi-dimensional beings."

Noah could sense the helplessness on Ryder's forlorn brow. "Come on, don't worry about it. Worry is like praying for a negative outcome. Right now is the only moment that matters. Let's go watch some home movies. Those always cheer you up. The one of that little girl's birthday party or the one of the parade in that small town before it cuts to a family opening presents on Christmas morning..."

"I just wish I had some sort of training for this. I feel unprepared."

"You don't realize it, but you've been training for this your entire life – just by being you. You're the magic ticket, the secret ingredient. You have the correct cosmic magnetic charge. Your soul is true. You're the one who can get the message through. When the Moynihans come in here and give us the word that it's time to roll, your instincts will tell you what to do. Always trust your instincts and follow your gut. The light is on you, don't be blue, your soul is true. When it's time, you're going to get on your bike and ride. We'll set your course in the GPS device we're adding to your bicycle. It will guide you through the forest and to the coast where Crystal and Grace live and work. They're in charge of the PERD."

"What's that?"

"The PERD – it stands for the 'Primary Environmental Restoration Division' of The People's People. By the people, for the people."

After Ryder and Noah finished enjoying the port, they retired to a room with the ambiance of being outside. One could dial in the environment or season of their choosing. They chose a cool summer's night with a hint of fall in the air.

"You feel that?" Noah asked. "I love the changing of the seasons. It'll be fall soon then winter."

Meanwhile, up on the planet's surface, the tornadic wind that had ripped and sucked Ryder into the vacuum of Noah Billingsworth's portal was still raging with the fierceness of an angry beast. A few soldiers and assassins of The Queen's army persevered, fighting the elements, searching for rumored clues floating around the kingdom that a suspicious person was lurking about, possibly associated with Noah Billingsworth. Noah and his secrets were safe at the moment. There was no evidence detected by The Queen's secret police that indicated where he was hiding. These soldiers searching the area where Ryder vanished were not the bulk of The Queen's forces. The largest mass of her forces was elsewhere – continuing their blitzkrieg, storming through the forest and villages, laying waste to the inhabitants within. But if Noah's hideaway were found, even a small party of soldiers could wreak havoc, alerting The Queen and ruining any chance of the plan being carried out. Besides the cosmic alignment that needed to occur before Ryder could start the journey, it was imperative that no soldiers or patrols were near the re-entry point of the space-time continuum portal outside Noah's hidden lair.

As they watched the surreal sky change colors, Noah said to Ryder, "Even if there's a patrol outside the portal when the optimum moment arrives for you to leave, we'll need to take our chances and send you on your journey anyway."

"Wow, that's a beautiful sunset! And you're right – the weather's perfect. I can taste fall in the air."

As the days and weeks went by inside Noah Billingsworth's suspended animation chamber, time stood still by comparison up on the Earth's surface. Delicious meals, insightful conversations, 8mm home movies, and Stravinsky's "The Rites of Spring," often immersed with Art Blakey or Charles Mingus, filled the days and nights. Noah shared philosophy and teachings from throughout the ages, preparing Ryder for the crucial journey ahead.

Half-drunk on wine one evening, Noah Billingsworth explained, rather philosophically, a thought from an ancient text, "Like a lotus flower rising from the warm mud near a stream, we also begin life in the mud, rising up out of the muck and mire to bloom in the sunshine, just as our spiritual journey brings us from ignorance to spiritual exploration to enlightenment. We must communicate these messages to Mars then back through our galaxy to save our planet. And that's why you must find Crystal."

Each within their own thoughts, both were silent, listening to the music emanating from the turntable.

Ryder broke the silence. "You've lived for so long down here – for centuries. And up on Earth, so much has changed. What's something you miss the most?"

"I miss the chatter of kids playing together in the neighborhood on a pleasant evening. Two other things I really miss are garage sales; some folks called them 'yard sales'. And I miss potlucks, or 'covered dish suppers,' as my grandparents from the South called them."

Ryder had never heard of these things. Noah could sense Ryder's confusion, so he tried clarifying by further explaining.

"You know what I really miss? The social interaction with everyday people. Fortunately, I *do* have Mrs. Gutridge, the Moynihans, and all the other staff and crew here, but I miss meeting strangers or hearing from an old friend. I miss those random, spontaneous encounters with people in one's day-to-day life that make it interesting and fun. It's such a shame that mankind can't figure out how to be kind to one another and to take care of each other and the planet."

Noah paused for a moment, both of them absorbed in their own thoughts, then continued explaining, "No matter who you are, no matter how smart or how dumb someone is, no matter how rich or poor, or how mean and cruel, or how nice and pleasant someone is, at some point in everyone's life, someone had to wipe our butts and change our diapers. That's something we all have in common."

Ryder smiled and nodded in agreement.

"You know where society failed?" Noah didn't wait for an answer. "It was when people refused to scrub their own floors."

After more silent inner-reflection, Billingsworth spoke. "Everything in the universe is sound and vibration. If the loss of harmony is so great that the vibration and the dissonance becomes fierce, the planet shatters. The great Vedic teachings tell us that we are one in eternal pure being. I have many books. I was reading the philosophy of a man named [illegible] and he was saying if we can unify everyone's thinking into realizing this, perhaps we can rid the world of the strife that causes greed, prejudice, and hatred. This love transforms life into a divine dance, the cosmic dance. The divine plan of the cosmic dance. The potential to transform a troubled world exists in the collective consciousness. Collective consciousness unites us. There resides the power for change. What could be more beautiful than a whole planet experiencing this as one? When the flow is lost, wholeness is lost. Think of how a tree grows. Everything is organized for one purpose, and that's to keep the tree alive and thriving. *That's* how we need to change as the human race. We need to do everything possible to keep all of us alive and thriving. If one person is doing well and so is the next person then we'll all be doing better. The better off each of us can be, the better off everyone can be – if we change our thinking. Every moment that you've been alive, every cell in your body has been focused on the single purpose of staying alive and thriving. The mind must join this process. If we can collectively get everyone's mind thinking on the same thing and at the same time, we can change the world together. And now, we've taken it a step further by figuring out ways to harness the brain's power and turn it into energy. If we combine specific individuals with specific mind and body elements, we'll be able to transmit a message to the colonies on Mars, requesting the specific elements we need for them to launch back to us here on Earth in order to reverse the domino effect of the recent destruction to the health and well-being of our planet. When the biorhythms of the body, mind, and spirit are in balance, we generate all the energy we need. That part of our brain we're just now learning to tap into. We call it the 'psychic transmitter'. The philosopher Aeschylus once said, 'From a small seed, a mighty trunk may grow.' And we have that seed – each and every one of us possesses that magic seed – inside our mind and within our spirit."

As Noah Billingsworth spoke, he noticed the lotus flowers growing from a container on the table. He reached out, gently touched one of the petals, and said, "The philanthropical English writer and lecturer from the 1800s, Clara Lucas Balfour, once said, 'Are not flowers the stars of the earth?'"

CHAPTER THIRTEEN

One evening, while playing board games with Ryder in the den, Noah Billingsworth said, "When I stopped being a child actor, I gave up childish ways, or so I thought. I just love playing with these old toys. This is a game called 'electric football'. You line up these plastic football players on this metal field and when you hit the switch, an electric current runs through it, vibrating the field, causing the pieces to jostle around until one of the defensive players touches the offensive player holding a little cotton football. It's so random and it takes forever before anything really happens. What amuses me is that this used to be entertaining to kids."

He picked up a box and proceeded to teach Ryder about board games. "This one is called 'Monopoly,' and it never gets old. Created during The Great Depression in America during the 1920s and 30s, it's a game of winner-takes-all, just like modern-day society…unless the player who is winning decides to show some mercy and cuts their opponents some slack."

CHAPTER FOURTEEN

Queen Daffodil's onslaught continued. Fortunately, for The People's People, she took her armored divisions through the easier passage, avoiding the mud pits, canyons, and gorge, which led them away from Crystal, Grace, and the PERD headquarters in The Crystal City. Still, The Queen's damage was catastrophic, cutting a massive swath through nature and the humble hamlets and dwellings that lay in her path. Bogged down in the natural terrain and unable to move her tanks and weaponry forward, The Queen sent operatives out into the villages to spread lies, deceit, and propaganda, pitting the modest peasants against themselves. Once the armor and troops were no longer able to roll into the towns, the brainwashed do-gooders made obvious who in the towns and villages were contrary to the regime, making the choices of which ones to torture easy and carefree. Citizens who escaped torture were less likely to fight back, having witnessed their peers being brutalized in public. Often, these individuals were turned into servants of The Queen. Many of them were beaten then used as slaves. The spoils to the victor were not to be taken lightly. The Queen's sexual appetite and perversion could rarely be quenched. She sexually tortured men, women, and children – many well past the point of death. Some were allowed to survive, just to be forced to endure unthinkable pain and suffering. Queen Daffodil was playing for keeps. And no one and no entity appeared to be anywhere close to matching wits or strengths with her. She had survived countless assassination attempts and had conquered every nation that stood in her way.

Jeremiah Moynihan rushed into the room, followed by his brother. Jeremiah habitually pushed his glasses back up his nose. He was sweating so profusely that the spectacles could barely stay on his face.

"We got…we gotta…we gotta get. We have to hurry!" he finally muttered emphatically, nearly out breath.

"What?" Billingsworth asked.

"We gotta move fast. We umm…we-we-we almost missed our spot."

"How?"

"Josh-for-brains here didn't put a decimal in the right place," Jeremiah answered, pointing to his brother.

"It wasn't a decimal. Sharon forgot to carry the one," replied Joshua.

"Well, it was YOUR staff member who missed it, and if Ross didn't figure it out..."

"Ross didn't catch it. It was our team member who caught it, but there's still plenty of time for Ryder to shoot the coop."

"Okay, both you guys settle down," Billingsworth directed. "Jeremiah, for God's sake, take a breath. You're so red in the face, I'm afraid you're gonna keel over."

Joshua giggled while adding, "Yeah, man. Take a breath, it's gonna be fine. Ryder, you ready for the ride of your life?"

Jeremiah started to relax and perked up when he began explaining the bike. "We totally cleaned up your bike."

"Did you put grease on the chain?" Ryder asked.

Joshua began laughing again as Jeremiah explained. "Oh, man! You won't recognize this thing. We disassembled it, retooled some of the parts, cleaned it up, oiled, polished, and replaced worn-out spokes, and yes...we greased your chain like you wouldn't believe."

Joshua piped up. "We equipped it with a GPS and an anti-cloaking device that will keep you, as best as possible, off any heat sensory radar or sonar device used by The Queen's regime. There's also a small force field that can be used moderately at times to shield you from bad weather."

"However, it won't last your entire journey. Because someone's team didn't realize that when using quantum physics complex numbers in the complex conduit…"

"Oh, stop it, will you? *Our* team…"

Noah interrupted the brotherly dispute. "Fellas, please. Don't fight in front of company."

The brothers went on to explain…

"We have special hydration and nutrition pills that are more developed than the stuff the government gives you. These are actually healthy, and they taste good."

"They really do."

"That's something we both agree on."

"These nutrition pills actually taste like Mrs. Gutridge's cooking!"

"Mmmmmmmm, they really do."

Noah chimed in. "One more thing that the Moynihans and their teams did for your safety: they added two weapons, but hopefully you won't have to use them. Two ray guns, one on the front of your bike and the other on the back. Each can shoot a ray that will spread wider as it travels, ensuring that you hit any militant you target."

"That's right," the Moynihans added in unison.

"These rays are capable of taking out quite a large number of predators at once."

"The only issue is you'll have limitations as to how often you can use it."

The Moynihans took turns finishing each other's sentences.

"It's self-restoring, though."

"That's right, it will replenish itself overtime."

"Yes, so if you have to use it."

"Hopefully, you'll finish off whoever's attacking you."

"Before you run out of juice."

"How much juice does it have?" Ryder asked.

The brothers Moynihan looked at each other, smiled, shrugged, and giggled.

"We don't know, exactly," Jeremiah replied, nudging his specs back up the bridge of his nose.

Through a slight stutter, he continued, "There should be plenty of juice in these puppies. We're just not totally sure about the duration of each ray gun."

CHAPTER FIFTEEN

Ryder was truly stunned when two young men in white lab coats wheeled out the bike. If not for a few decals that were on the bike when it was found, Ryder might not have recognized that it was the same bicycle. A young woman, also in a white lab coat, walked toward Ryder, beaming with pride as she offered a special and unique bicycle helmet.

"This helmet," Joshua explained, "is probably the most complex apparatus we've made for your journey."

"You need to wear this special jumpsuit, too," Jeremiah directed.

"Yes, the two work in congruence with each other."

"That's right. They have a cloaking device on them."

"They can also project a 3D image of the maps."

"And high-altitude videos of your surroundings."

"That can be zoomed into near-microscopic detail."

"The helmet and suit combined have a special shield."

"That can protect you from most any of the elements."

"And almost any temperatures."

"That exist on Earth."

"It will not protect you from the sub-zero temperatures from outer space, though."

"We're not launching anyone into outer space."

"I know that. I'm just mentioning it."

Billingsworth cleared his throat, glanced toward Ryder, smiled, and reminded the Moynihans, "Please, fellows – our guest."

The Moynihans discussed with Ryder the finer details of every aspect of every bit of information pertaining to the suit, helmet, and bicycle, as well as what to expect on the journey, including the cosmic re-entry. They also reviewed the intricacies of the formulas and equations Ryder was to share with Crystal and Grace. They gave instructions about the maps and which route to take on the trip. Finally, after all was said and done, they launched Ryder, who was adorned in the new jumpsuit with the high-tech helmet and bicycle, back into the old, yet current dimension.

By the time the explanations wrapped up, there wasn't a lot of moments left for goodbyes. Noah assured Ryder that they would see each other again either in person or through some sort of technological device, but not to worry. As the four of them approached the evacuation chambers, the Moynihans each produced a pair of vintage aviation goggles – similar to the ones worn by pilots from the early 1900s – and strapped them around their faces. Noah Billingsworth applied a much more modern version of eye protection, something that looked like two slices of cucumber, but he could see through them.

"These are great!" he exclaimed. "Not only can I see through them, but they also work like telescoping binoculars. And they help to shrink the bags under my eyes."

"Don't I need some sort of eye protection?" Ryder asked.

"No, the force field created by your suit and helmet will protect your eyes from any particles in the hurricane-force wind as you re-enter Earth's time field. They will help you see clearly through any matter that might be clogging the airways."

"How will I know where to go if something does go wrong with the GPS on the helmet?"

"Many paths lead to the same destination; it doesn't matter how you get there. The unknown is where all things and all outcomes are possible. Listen to the whispers of the universe. From a small seed, a mighty trunk may grow. You're like the cosmic Johnny Appleseed. You're Ryder Appleseed. You can do this! You *will* do this. I've been watching you for a long time. I know you, Ryder. I'm going to miss you when you're gone, but we'll meet again. I know we will meet again."

After Ryder was launched into the former timeline, Noah Billingsworth became melancholy and slightly despondent.

He retired to his den and sat alone, listening to the song "Naima" by John Coltrane. Each time the song ended, Noah would lift up the needle on the phonograph and gently set it back in the groove at the top of the record. He listened to the haunting melody over and over again until he finally drifted off to sleep.

CHAPTER SIXTEEN

Re-entry was even crazier and more difficult than Ryder had imagined. Little time had elapsed from being sucked into the vacuum of the suspended animation chamber until the very second Ryder and the bicycle crossed over their own shadow from the exact moment they had disappeared. The soldiers that had been giving chase were still in the vicinity, but were now oblivious to Ryder, thanks to the well-equipped bicycle and helmet with its cloaking device.

The air was raging with chaos and debris. Gale-force winds blew hard, making maneuvering the bike tedious and difficult. Ryder managed to cut a path and locked into an airstream that carried the newly enlightened traveler out of the thick forest and harsh weather and into an open meadow. The meadow smelled of sweet, fragrant flowers. Ryder's improved bike was effortless to pedal. The gears could still be operated by hand, but they changed automatically at each opportune moment. Ryder had never breathed air so fresh. There were many species of birds floating around the sky and small furry creatures frolicked about.

Suddenly, the temperature changed, and darkness began to color the horizon. The acidic smell of sulfur filled the air. Lightning crackled with intense ferocity. Directly in front of Ryder's path, about 200 yards away, a cloud of disturbance swirled about. It was caused by a huge mob of boots charging forward, each pair of boots carrying arms of destruction. From behind, Ryder could feel the vibration and hear the clatter of large weaponry – massive weapons of destruction – rolling in from the distance. Turning to look, Ryder noticed the cloud was growing in size; it was still farther off in the distance, but was getting closer and gathering momentum.

The stampeding soldiers. It wouldn't be long before they would be upon Ryder and the bike.

Using the radar and telescope on the helmet and suit, Ryder could safely assess that the soldiers and machinery were charging in on this path with a purpose. Listening to instincts and the whispers of the universe, Ryder turned and rode to the east. Crystal and Grace were in the opposite direction, but Ryder didn't want to lead the forces toward them, and instead, found a gully to ride in to escape. The gully followed the slope of a hill. As it transcended downward, mounds of earth rose on either side of the path, forming dunes that provided protection from the advancing army's view. Soon, the gully became a path for a trickle of water. The trench was becoming deeper within the towering walls of earth, which rose vertically and shot straight up into the air. It wasn't apparent where the water was coming from, but as Ryder road further along, it became obvious. There was no easy way to turn around.

The trickle grew into a small stream and began rising an inch or two above the bike's wheel line. The protective force field around the bicycle kept Ryder dry. The stream continued to increase in size and strength…soon, the force of the current became so strong, it couldn't be fought. Ryder was pressed to surrender to its overwhelming power, going with the flow and steering the best one could under these circumstances. Even with the technology of the helmet, visibility was very limited.

The path and current became more difficult to maintain. Ryder felt as though the bike was beginning to float. The water was choppy, tossing the buoyant bicycle around like a cork bobbing in a storm. Large bits of debris and tree limbs smashed into the shield of the bike. The rush and roar of the water grew louder. Alarm systems inside the jumpsuit and helmet began to flash, setting off a series of beeps and a siren moments before plummeting over the edge of a towering waterfall.

Knocked unconscious from the splashdown landing, it was apparent that the special suit and helmet kept Ryder alive. However, the technology and equipment had been damaged in the fall. Water started leaking through the suit and into the helmet, waking up Ryder. Still holding on to the bike, and now floating down a river, Ryder knew it was imperative to reach land and find a hiding place to regroup. Relieved of the bike's buoyant abilities, Ryder partly pedaled and partly paddled over to the bank. Quickly finding cover behind some overgrown brush forming tall hedgerows along the banks of the river, Ryder set the bike down. Ryder had never been in water so clean. The meadow, the dunes, the mounds of earth, the river, were the cleanest nature ever witnessed. It was almost as if this were a different planet. Nothing like this was even close to the life known in the city, or even the countryside around the city where Ryder grew up. Even the forest where the adventure with Noah Billingsworth had unfolded was not as pristine as this place.

After a brief recuperation, Ryder picked up the bike, and forged through thick brush for what seemed like miles until abruptly arriving at a cliff wall. Long vines hung down the wall of the cliff. Looking up, Ryder noticed an overhanging solid sheet of stone jetting out above what appeared to be an enclave inserted into the wall about 35 feet up. Ryder attached a vine around and through the frame of the bike. Then, grabbing onto another set of limbs, proceeded to scale the side of the cliff, reaching the landing with relative ease. Ryder then hoisted up the bike with the twisted ropes of growth attached to the frame of the bike. The dirt landing was a clay floor that sat at an angle, making it easy to hide behind its crest. It was obvious that heavy rain would bring water into the opening of what turned out to be a very deep cave. This would provide ample safety for the time being while a new plan was devised to locate Crystal and Grace in an attempt to complete this cosmic mission.

The floor and walls of the cave were made of clay, packed tightly. Ryder's investigation through an opening inside the cave proved three separate chambers, two of which were deeper into the cave than the first. The opening of the cave faced west, and even though it was well hidden by the berm and some tall trees, the sun shone fairly deep into the openings of the cave, lighting all the chambers with natural light. Against the wall in the forward chamber, dark soot ran up the side of the wall, darkening the curved ceiling of the cave – indications that someone had used this spot, possibly hundreds of years prior, for a fire. Inside both of the other chambers, Ryder discovered some drawings and primitive artwork along the walls. Parietal art and petroglyphs.

On the back wall of the third chamber, Ryder discovered a crevice through which another opening led to a fourth massive, circular cathedral-sized room partially lit by sunlight entering through an opening at the top of the ceiling. In the center of the naturally formed room, there was a giant geoglyph. The petroform was a medicine wheel made by the First Nation tribes over a thousand years ago. Not knowing exactly what this was, Ryder couldn't help but feel the vibrations, the power of the ancient spirits still looking out over the holy remains. Pausing to say a prayer of thanks and another for protection in the upcoming journey, Ryder could hear the whispers of the universe. Ryder eased back through the opening in the crevasse back into the other portions of the cave.

Meanwhile, Queen Daffodil ventured to her palace. Fuming with anger, she could sense the presence of a threat, of a being or some sort of energy, by which she felt threatened. Whatever this was, it was something she knew she needed to deal with. She called in the members of her Cabinet, executing people on the spot if they seemed unsure of what she meant when she brought up the invisible threat. The marble floor was blood soaked and littered with the bodies of disemboweled senators, generals, and department heads. New appointees quickly learned to play along, placating the enraged ruler. Of course, if The Queen felt falsely kowtowed to, she would execute them, too. As of late, there were so many executions that The Queen no longer took pleasure in it. No time for prolonged torture and sexual rage. She was preoccupied with the overwhelming feeling that the counterpart equal to her in intelligence, psychological wit, mental fortitude, and strength was nearby on the planet's surface.

After recovering for a couple of days inside the cave, Ryder set out on an exploration of the surrounding area. Approaching a brook, Ryder could hear voices through the woods, as well as the undeniable sound of laughter and water splashing around. Ryder dismounted and approached on foot, quietly pushing the bike along a path until two individuals could be seen playing in the still water of a stream. It was such an unusual sensation to see people playing in water. Where Ryder was from, even if you found a body of water, it wouldn't be safe to get into it.

Peeking over a shrub, Ryder could see two young nymphs standing in shallow water reaching just below their naked breasts. Playfully splashing each other with the water and completely unaware of being spied upon, the two seemed fearless, yet vulnerable. Leaning forward to get a better look at the nakedness in the clear water, a twig snapped under the front tire of the bike.

"Who's that? Who's there?" one of the maidens inquired.

"We can see you. Come over here, you coward!" the other one snapped.

"Hello. I'm sorry. I didn't mean to frighten you," Ryder replied…although it was Ryder who was frightened and who felt threatened. "I was just out scouting around, and I happened upon you. Do you live around here?"

"What's it to you?" the second one snapped again at Ryder.

"Mary Beth, please," the first one begged. "Let's show the young traveler some courtesy. They look lost and I don't believe you pose any threat to us…do you?" she asked, gently looking into Ryder's eyes.

"Oh, no. As a matter of fact, I don't think I pose a threat to anyone. I mean, I don't…pose a threat. I don't care to harm anyone. I'm on a mission. A mission of peace," Ryder stated, unsure if that last part should be mentioned, but felt as though these two were trustworthy and not a threat to the mission.

"What's your name?"

"My name is Ryder."

"Hello, Ryder. My name is Tabatha, and this is Mary Beth. Say hello, Mary Beth."

"Hello," Mary Beth said before continuing, "sorry if I seemed bitchy a minute ago, but you gotta be careful out here. There are some evildoers roaming about!"

"I'm well aware. That's why I was surprised to see you both playing so carefree in the water. Also, I'm not used to being in a place where the water is safe to drink or touch, much less to splash around in."

"You should jump in! If you've never lived in a place where it's safe to jump into the water, you will die! I mean, it won't kill you. You're gonna freak out. You'll love it!"

"It feels amazing, Ryder. You should get in."

Intrigued, but not feeling completely safe in this environment, Ryder hesitated.

"I'll pass for now. I fell into a stream over a waterfall a few miles back a couple of days ago and that was enough for me. So, do you live in these woods?"

Before they could answer, the sound of a drone flying overhead stopped both young ladies from answering.

"We should leave – quickly!" Tabatha exclaimed.

"We can hide in the cave I found. It's not too far away," suggested Ryder.

"No, it would be safer if you came with us. We have a place nearby that will be safe for you to hide until the drones are done surveying the area."

The maidens led the way to a thatched hut hidden

amongst a cluster of cypress trees and old-growth redwoods. The hut was only a short distance from the brook.

Ryder was made to feel comfortable, and the three of them spent many days living with and getting to know each other. Mary Beth and Tabatha taught Ryder about the plants in the woods, the ones that were safe to eat and the ones with medicinal purposes. They taught Ryder how to forage the forest floor to find mushrooms and truffles that were nourishing and unharmful. Ryder learned how to dig for tubers and roots that were a healthy food source. They picked leaves and mint, along with other herbs and spices for making tinctures and teas. They sat up late at night watching the stars or lounging on pillows on the floor of the hut, each reminiscing of their pasts, their childhoods, and the recent encounters with the regime under Queen Daffodil and her evil forces. Ryder was pleased to find out that Mary Beth and Tabatha knew of Crystal and Grace. They were also part of The People's People movement to regain the planet – to save the hope that humanity can still live by the people, for the people. Mary Beth and Tabatha had been doing their part; along with the assistance of other women and men like themselves, they were out to help save mankind and the planet.

As the three continued to get to know each other, they began showing signs of affection for one another, eventually taking turns sharing love and being amorous with one another. Ryder had had very little human contact with people while living back in the desolate city. Life was hard and difficult, with barely any time or attention given to anything other than survival. The warm embrace of touch and skin had healing powers to a person so lonely once before.

After spending several days in their wooded Shangri-La of cypress trees and ancient redwoods, Tabatha, Mary Beth, and Ryder knew it was time for the journey to commence. The journey to the encampment where Crystal and Grace held fort.

Trained with new skills and the knowledge of how to forage and live off the land, Ryder was well fortified and equipped for the task at hand. To aid in the journey, the two nature goddesses recommended Ryder make use of a trusted troglodyte they knew – a nemophilist to act as a guide into and through the secret Mosaic Forest. Just on the other side of the great crevasse, they would find the encampment of The People's People.

"We have a wise and trusted associate who can ensure a safer passage for you rather than you traveling alone to your destinations," Tabatha said.

"I've always imagined I'd do this journey alone, and I wonder if it'd be safer if only one person were sneaking about. Less energy to detect if The Queen were to send her drones looking for suspect travelers..."

"It's for the best if he travels with you. His name is Paraffin, and he's a celestial being who has lived on Earth for many centuries. He is a wise, intuitive soul. He knows these woods and The Mosaic Forest better than anyone who has walked the Earth. He's a sage with profound strength and fortitude. We will signal for him tonight and he should arrive before two crows caw."

"You won't make it traveling alone," Mary Beth added.

Ryder agreed. Just as Tabatha and Mary Beth predicted, Paraffin showed up before the second crow cawed. The celestial being's sobriquet suited him to a T. He was a man with translucent oily skin, and he reeked of kerosene and polish. Ryder seemed surprised; the man appeared out of shape. Age wore on his face. He carried a staff made from twisted pieces of cypress wood that wound around itself. Dressed in a burlap garment stitched into a robe, he wore sandals on his feet that were held together by vines. Nothing about his get-up said 'swift traveler'. Ryder, sitting atop the retrofitted bicycle with a helmet and jumpsuit that were tricked out with the utmost technology, was an odd juxtaposition next to Paraffin.

After an awkward silence following the initial introduction, Ryder couldn't resist asking, "Do you have a bicycle or any other form of transportation? I imagined that we'd both be traveling in a swift and stealth manner."

"Swift and stealth are relative and meaningless if we're detected by The Queen and her henchman. We'll travel with the utmost care and crafty nature of any of the forest creatures surviving in this environment," Paraffin said.

Seeing the look of doubt on Ryder's face, Paraffin added, "Fear not, my vernal messenger. I will not hold us back by traveling afoot."

"Before you leave, we have these blessings…tokens to bestow upon you," Tabatha stated.

She placed a garland of flowers around each of their

necks then kissed them lightly on each cheek. Mary Beth followed with a burning clump of sage, wafting the smoke toward both of them. Tabatha offered these words from an ancient Chinese proverb:

May your life be simple and pure
so you know only beauty.
May your mind be clear and quiet
so you speak only truth.
May your heart be filled with love and compassion
so you radiate light to all you meet.
May all you do be blessed with Divine grace.

"Remember to listen to the whispers of the universe," Mary Beth directed. "Let them guide you."

They said their goodbyes and gave each other another round of hugs and kisses before the odd-looking pair walked out from the thatched hut, the cypress trees, and the old-growth redwoods. With the morning sun at their backs, Ryder and Paraffin walked to the path that would eventually lead them to The Mosaic Forest.

Ryder started off pedaling on the bike, but dismounted after a short distance. Looking back through the splintered sunlight, the thatched hut was a dim silhouette etched in eternity in the mind. Paraffin walked with a steady gait, long strides transversing the path with the grace of air, barely leaving a footprint or trace with each step. He spoke with a quiet and soothing tone, a pleasant timbre setting off no alarm to any creature near or far. Ryder knew immediately that there was a certain safety and assurance to the old man's persona. A feeling of thankfulness and gratitude came over the young traveler.

Paraffin wore a small pouch tied around his neck by a thin strap of leather. The pouch carried a crystal and some special herbs, along with dried flowers to thwart unwanted spirits. He had other tidbits of usefulness tucked away here and there, sewn up in little pockets hidden about his burlap robe. Special items were hidden up his sleeves and sewn into the hems of his robe: pieces of flint for starting fires, a small compass, bits of protein and vitamin capsules, supplements for trance and astral projection, medicines, some tools, and a special substance Paraffin called 'honey'.

Honey was a sweet concoction fortified with hyper-nutrients and an organic stimulant closely resembling a pure, high-octane amphetamine, only completely natural and derived from a root akin to sarsaparilla. Besides hyper-alertness, it gave the user the ability of clean, pure energy and focus without prolonged addictive qualities, and it didn't possess any damaging elements to the body. It was to be used only in extreme cases of endurance for survival or when under attack. If life or death depended on staying alert, focused, and clearheaded for days at a time, honey was extremely useful. Like anything, it couldn't go on forever. But these organic ingredients were derived from the concept and need for airplane pilots to stay alert for flights lasting longer than 24 hours during wartime, such as the long bomber missions from the mid- to late-2400s. Also, since the beginning of time, people, shamans, holy tribal leaders, and indigenous medicine men have been using natural substances to incite visions and trances in search of enlightenment.

Paraffin spoke to Ryder in a soft, low amble. "If there's ever a time we need to separate, if by chance we happen upon soldiers or threatening individuals or bandits, follow your instincts and flee as you may. I'll track you down and find you. As a matter of fact, if we ever do need to separate, I'll never be far away. With your cloaking device on your helmet and bike, you should be able to lose any small party of soldiers; it's the larger fleets of tanks and drones I worry about. Those may be able to spot you since they're equipped with more sophisticated forms of radar and detection devices."

Ryder nodded and asked, "How do you plan to stay safe and hidden? You're only equipped with a burlap robe."

"I have my ways, my young cosmic bicycle messenger. My translucent skin, along with the natural fibers that I wear, keep me relatively invisible to radar and heat-seeking screening. I tend to blend into my surroundings. Don't be alarmed if I suddenly disappear. If I sense anything peculiar or off, I'm liable to quickly fade into the environment until the coast is clear or the perceived threat is subdued or rendered harmless. But fear not, I'm like a human chameleon; I may be standing only a meter or two away from you. I'm not hiding to abandon you or from fear of being harmed. I may appear passive, but I'm capable of great feats of force and defense. I have the ability to attack and subdue any number of predators."

Paraffin's speech had such a pleasant drawl that Ryder was almost lulled to sleep listening to him. His voice was so soothing. Soon, the terrain and landscape began to change. The woods became a magical, multicolored forest. The bark of the trees was like none Ryder had ever seen or imagined. It had the glint and glimmer of polychromatic tortoise shells, rainbow pearl reflective wood. As the sun moved across the sky, rainbow prisms sent rays of effervescent colors gleaming off the woody bark, crowding a person's eyeballs, causing them to squint. Large rocks encrusted with gemstones of every color imaginable littered the forest floor. Vibrant, fluorescent-colored birds flew about when not gathered in vast numbers among the trees. A fragrant breeze wafted through the air of the evergreens, saturating the senses with delight.

"I never knew anything like this existed. I've never even heard of this place."

"This is The Mosaic Forest. It's been here since the days of Moses, thousands and thousands of years ago."

"How come I've never heard of it?"

"It's been obscured by an electromagnetic force field, rendering it unseeable, impenetrable, and non-detectable by any device known to mankind."

"How do you know about this place?"

"My family was left behind on Earth during the ancient times…before the great pyramids were born."

"Wait, what? Left behind on Earth? Before the pyramids were born?"

"The galaxy where I'm from, that's how we think of

things. It's an idea first before it's a reality, and that idea has to be born, or it is born. Even before it happens, or as the thought is being conceived, it is also being born. Who isn't being born is busy being conceived."

"So, where is your family from?"

"We're from an existence many time warps away. We're not just from another galaxy – that's much too linear. We're from many time warps away, from a world that isn't even in your timeline. Time bends, ebbs, and flows, like elastic. Occasionally, there's a burp or hiccup that causes brief holes in the balloons or soap bubbles that we all exist within…and that's what happened. We had a fleet of ships slip through a space fart into your world several thousand years ago. I was only a small infant at the time. Originally, on my family's spaceship, I was an experiment. I came from a petri dish. I eventually grew into in amphibious tadpole that took shape as a young humanoid in form by the time my family and the fleet of ships were sucked into your solar system's vortex."

"Did everyone survive the transition? How many of you are still alive? Are you still in contact with each other? How are *you* still alive?"

Before Ryder could get an answer, Paraffin disappeared, vanishing into the fabric of the scenery around them. Ryder soon realized why when two sentries on hovercrafts called out.

"Halt! Who goes there?"

Alarmed by the sudden intrusion, Ryder bore down hard and fast on the pedals, pointing the bike away from the ensuing voices before engaging the cloaking device on the suit and helmet. Electrical sound waves filled the air as laser shots rang out, disintegrating rocks and tree trunks, sending the large, multicolored goliaths to the ground. After engaging the cloaking device, Ryder doubled back around on the hovercraft, sneaking up behind the soldiers in a clandestine manner. Losing sight of their target, the two hovercrafts split apart, taking separate courses in an attempt to search a wider swath of land. But before they could separate, Ryder fired off a fortunate shot from the forward cannon on the bike, managing to hit and destroy the one hovercraft, which exploded and destroyed the second hovercraft in the process. Paraffin reappeared moments after the dual explosion.

"Nice shootin' there. I was getting ready to make an offensive maneuver myself, but you did a splendid job of taking care of business. It's possible they were already in radio contact with their command post before entering the forest. Fortunately, we can assume that they weren't able to transmit any messages to anyone once inside The Mosaic Forest. The electromagnetic particles that the gemstones and trees transfer into the atmosphere render communication devices obsolete."

"That's a relief!"

"Yeah, but we aren't out of the woods yet, so to speak. If those two were in contact with their superiors, or if anyone knew where they were on their patrol, they'll suspect foul play when they don't return. It's a bit of a fluke they were able to enter the protective force field of The Mosaic Forest to begin with. They must've accidentally slipped through a vibration in the wavelength after we passed through."

"What should we do?"

Paraffin quickly answered, "Well, no use worrying about it. There are some things we can't control. Most likely, they weren't able to send radio transmissions out of The Mosaic Forest due to the electrical frequencies that protect it. We should just be mindful and continue on our way. We shouldn't lose faith. They cannot defeat us. We must persevere!"

CHAPTER SEVENTEEN

Queen Daffodil was livid. Her pasty, yellow skin turned red with anger, coloring her cheeks with hues of orange. She stomped and cussed around the palace floors while continuing to slurp down ladles of rue. Rue was a fermented concoction of distilled alcohol mixed with the brine of barbed hornshell, a pungent fruit grown until overripe and rotten; and lastly, the mixture was poured over forkelberries. These berries had the consistency of deer feces, but when bitten into, were charcoal grey with the smeary texture of raccoon poop – quite the delicacy to The Queen. Much like caviar and crackers, she ate them by the spoonful on thin, crispy wafers made from the skin of her ensnared human victims. She delighted in the powerfully strong, bitter, foul, and intoxicating beverage that she consumed at a temperature between 90 and 96°C. The rue was kept bubbling in a vat. The Queen consumed its slimy ooze, slurping down ladle after ladle, parts of which dripped from the sides of her mouth.

"Goddammit, that's good rue! Now somebody get me my secretary to the interior and exterior. I need my overland, underland, and my para-national generals – every fucking one of them – in here, immediately, standing at attention before me. Do you hear me?" she yelled.

The court jester, who was sent in earlier to try and lighten the mood, wet himself then proceeded to drop his balls. Trying to pick them up and juggling while humming a simple circus ditty in between telling puns, he was soon put to death with the slashing of his throat.

"Now that's amusing," Queen Daffodil cackled while holding her chalice of rue underneath the jester's bleeding neck, adding fresh blood to her drink.

With every ladle of rue, The Queen grew more and more furious and perturbed. She was so drunk and mad with venom that she didn't notice when two more jesters were sent in through the drapery of the parlor entryway. Both of them weeping, already expecting death.

"Excuse me, Your Majesty," the palace corporal had returned from summoning the generals and secretaries that Her Highness petitioned.

"Your Highness, all but one of your generals are out in the field; they embarked on the mission of locating the Earth hounds and their leaders. Especially the mighty one that you speak of, the one you've sensed with your psychic abilities."

"This mighty one hasn't triggered my sensory field lately, but sooner or later, this being will be found out, I can promise you that. I'll put my hand on the Zell and swear by it."

Numb from drinking up ladles full of scalding hot rue and tired from disgust, Queen Daffodil screamed, "Who is responsible for this? The rue is cooling and turning into fondue!"

The maître d' in charge of food and beverages specifically for The Queen, fearful for his life and the lives of his family, pushed one of the kitchen interns out onto the floor to check on matters.

"Well!" she demanded, one eye looking at the corporal, the other eye at the intern.

Neither knew what to do or how to respond. Finally, the intern meekly spoke.

"I'm sorry, Your Majesty."

The corporal followed with, "Both of your secretaries are at luncheons, but they've been sent for and should arrive here shortly. General Gaughinlas and Colonel Carwrimes are also on their way and should arrive any moment now."

General Gaughinlas and Colonel Carwrimes's footsteps echoed down the marble corridor leading to Queen Daffodil's chambers. They arrived wearing polished calvary boots with pleated britches tucked inside them. Medallions dangled on both sides of the breast of their dress uniforms. A hush fell over the room as the officers walked into the parlor.

"Your Majesty, we arrived as quickly as possible."

"Thank God," she said before adding, "this rue is ruined. It's too cold. Don't ever try to reheat rue."

Queen Daffodil lifted a wooden saber above her head, and with her other hand, she pointed an onyx wand toward the intern, disintegrating him in a flash with a laser beam of energy. There was the lingering smell of flesh and sulfur as the micro-dust from the intern's remains glistened in a dance, like a billion tiny fireflies in the rays of light from the setting sun shining through the westward windows.

The corporal didn't flinch, which probably saved his life. Seemingly unaffected, he went on with the business at hand.

"May I present General Gaughinlas and Colonel Carwrimes."

The corporal saluted, curtsied, and clicked his heels together three times as he did an about-face before marching out of the room.

"General Gaughinlas," The Queen stated, but before continuing, she stumbled and grabbed the arm of her throne. Turning her head, she vomited on the floor then barked, "Bring me more rue, goddammit!"

Straightening back to an upright position, she asked, "General Gaughinlas, why have I not received word yet on anything?"

General Gaughinlas began to stammer. The Queen didn't wait for him to find his tongue.

"There have been no updates. Nothing. Nada. Not even the teeniest, tiniest hint of a lead as to the whereabouts of the nonsensical capital of The People's People, the location of their city, or their command center."

There was a brief, but infinite pause of silence before Queen Daffodil spoke again.

"Who should I hold responsible?"

She didn't move, but the officers felt crippled by the stare she gave them. Like a crazed lizard, each of her eyes moved independently of one another in any and every direction.

She repeated herself, "Who should I hold accountable for this? We have the greatest technology and knowledge in the solar system."

This wasn't entirely true, but she liked to think so. She continued with her tirade, "And we can't find a bunch of cosmic ecological vagabonds? There's gonna be hell to pay! God help me, Saint Wilkmeed!"

Attempting to get out a few words of reason, General Gaughinlas said, "With all due respect—"

But that was as far as he got before The Queen interrupted.

"Goddammit, this is the negligence of someone! Even if I don't punish the ones who are to blame, I'm going to punish somebody if it hairlips the Pope. Now, who's it going to be? One of you? Or should I punish one of the incompetents commanding the troops?"

"Well, Your Highness—" General Gaughinlas tried once again, but was interrupted.

"Is it you? Should I torture and kill you or this weasel here?" Queen Daffodil turned to look at Colonel Carwrimes.

General Gaughinlas stood erect with his chin up, clicked

his heels together, and bravely said, "I hold the responsibility of your worship. You can hold me accountable."

"Fine," Queen Daffodil agreed. "So be it! String up the colonel."

Her henchmen, who wore studded leather masks and lead-ringed armored vests, entered The Queen's chambers. Bearing leather straps and chains, they proceeded to tie up and chain Colonel Carwrimes to the shackles on the wall.

"But I'm the one responsible!" General Gaughinlas exclaimed. "Don't torture and kill Colonel Carwrimes. He's a good soldier and a faithful family man. Spare him and punish me. I'm his sup—"

Queen Daffodil raised her wooden saber and said, "That's right, you're his superior. So, you're the one who's going to suffer the most by watching me torture and kill your underling."

The Queen turned her entire mammoth frame without turning her neck or moving either eye so that she was directly facing Colonel Carwrimes.

She asked him, "So, you're a family man?"

"Yes, ma'am."

"How many kids do you have?"

"I've got six children, Your Lordship, and my wife is currently pregnant with twins."

"Good Lord! You're about to have eight kids to care for?"

"Yes, ma'am. That's correct."

"Well, I'm sorry to hear that. Strip off his clothes," she directed the henchmen.

The mob of henchmen proceeded to slice off Colonel Carwrimes's garments. Some of them paused in between the task to unfasten the medals and insignias, looking very apelike as they turned them over in their hands while peering through slits in their leather masks. The colonel began to fidget and protest, drawing two swift fists to the face from the largest of the masked henchmen. The others continued dividing up the pins and medals, taking turns attaching them to each other's vests. One more bout of fists to the face and torso ensued from each of the henchmen before they finished slicing and removing all but a few shreds of the officer's uniform. If not for being attached to the wall, Colonel Carwrimes would've collapsed to the floor. He was held up by the chains and straps mounted in the stone wall. Mouth bleeding, welts and bruises rose on his face and torso, naked for all to see.

Queen Daffodil took a serious analysis of her prey. She looked him up and down, head to toe, before waddling over closer to him. She took another look up and down, with each eye moving on its own accord. Her scaling face let out a burst. One loud cackle and half her mouth turned upward in a grin.

Pointing her wooden saber at his groin, she asked, "Is this your babymaker? Is this what the good Lord gave you to make eight goddamn children with?"

She began to laugh. A genuine laugh. The soldiers standing at attention along the chamber walls – always armed, always on guard, always standing by, waiting for her beck and call – couldn't believe their ears. Many of the soldiers were without souls or a conscience, but some of them knew Queen Daffodil was sick and needed to be brought to justice, yet here they stood by and did nothing. Disgusted yet afraid of retribution, they were simply cowards.

"This, this here is it? This is your babymaker? Oh, my word! How does something so tiny manage to make this man a papa?"

The wooden saber had a razor-sharp edge. With the tip of this deadly weapon, she attempted to lift the tip of the colonel's tiny penis. She bent over slightly to peer underneath it. Then, with one fell swoop, she turned and sliced off a quarter of General Gaughinlas's face.

"Throw the general into the dungeon! You can take this naked procreator and throw him out of the palace."

She turned, looked at Colonel Carwrimes, and said, "Before I let you go, I want you to understand…I better see some goddamn fucking results – and pronto! As much as I'd love to destroy your happy home by taking all of those children and turning them into my dinner, I think by letting you live, I'll see some results. If not, I'll make veal out of your unborn twins."

Blood washed onto the floor as General Gaughinlas was ushered out of the chamber and down to the dungeon. Blood poured from his face, leaving a dark red trail along the way.

The Queen hollered out for the maître d', "Gather up the general's face off the floor. I'll have that for dinner, lightly seared and served with more rue, at once…or you're going to be cut up and made into chum for the Dire Wolves!"

CHAPTER EIGHTEEN

While in hiding, Crystal and Grace continued running their lab work, analyses, and experiments around the clock. Today, they were analyzing moss to detect the percentages of plastics and pollutants that were within the plant's DNA. Fortunately, the numbers were on the decline. The moss showed less contaminants than just six months to a year prior.

Word reached the city fortress that The Queen had returned to her hidden palace and only small units remained out on patrol in regions far from The Crystal City. Lookouts in treetop towers lining the coast and along the perimeters of the gorge kept a vigilant watch day and night. Plugged into sonic receptors and using old fashioned binoculars, as well as solar radar, they continuously scanned the horizons in all directions 24 hours a day.

The People's People were out on patrol, too. They were keeping tabs on their surroundings in case any reconnaissance mission by the evil Queen's henchmen made it through undetected. The Crystal City's community was getting back to some sort of normalcy, with people going about their daily activities and duties to restore the planet. Still, tension was in the air. Burdened by the strain of being on constant guard of an impending assault, everyone still remained hopeful.

Just after lunch, Crystal and Grace were interrupted from their analysis of moss by a messenger summoning them to the radio tower. Several important messages had arrived from three different sources. The transcript had been decoded and it was imperative for Crystal and Grace to receive the information immediately.

An intern from the radio room walked into the lab, stood at attention, and announced, "Excuse the interruption, ma'am. We've received several important messages from different sources in the last few minutes. The messages are being decoded at this very moment and both of you need to come with me to the radio room right away."

The messages were cryptic information pertaining to a person named Ryder, along with the ancient being, Paraffin. The duo was on its way with vital information needed to save the planet. The messages explained (without being completely clear) that this person, Ryder, was bringing a formula, an equation that would allow them to transmit a message through outer space to the colonies on Mars. The transcript went on to say, '*We can only hope that life on Mars has been more successful in the last 150 years than here on Earth.*' And it was signed by Noah Billingsworth.

A second message from Tabatha and Mary Beth was less detailed. It stated that Ryder was in route with the ancient celestial soul, Paraffin, and their arrival could be expected within a week or more, depending on any difficulties they might encounter along the way.

And the third message from Paraffin was brief. It read:

Currently transversing The Mosaic Forest.
Encountered a patrol of two.
Subdued and rendered nonexistent.
On our way.

This message gave Crystal and Grace cause for alarm. Hopefully, this was only a fluke for two henchmen to be near or to have transcended the magical shield of The Mosaic Forest. It was possible that they snuck through an opening, briefly left behind after Paraffin parted the shield for Ryder and him to go through. If, for some reason, Queen Daffodil had discovered the secret of the existence of The Mosaic Forest and if they were now able to transcend its hidden realm at will, it would put The Crystal City and all of the restorative work to the environment in grave danger.

Lastly, a fourth message from an unknown source said the following and was accompanied by a simple drawing:

I am on a linear track.
You are a wavelength.
Our paths will only cross at certain junctures.

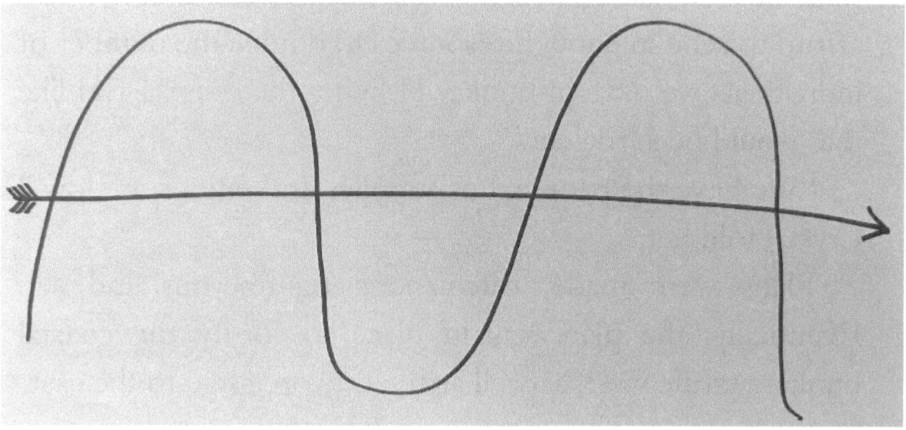

"I want to thank you guys for your swift action in receiving and discerning the transcript and getting us this information quickly," Crystal said. "We should keep the caution level at code red."

Pulling down a map fastened to an old projector screen attached to the ceiling, she continued her orders.

"Prepare the anti-assault team. Have them deploy units to reach quadrants G, H, and I. We're going to reinforce the line overlooking the canyon. They need to dig in and be given full rations to last for up to three weeks."

Using a slim pointer, she tapped on the ~~right~~ left edge of the map outlining the coast and explained, "Because of her aversion to water, I don't expect an amphibious landing, but we can't afford to take anything for granted."

Turning to Grace, Crystal asked, "What do you think? How many people and how much of our resources should we allocate to guarding the coastal regions?"

Grace responded, "I agree that our resources are spread thin, but we can't leave the coast unprotected. If we can afford to send in enough resources to double the number of individuals we have in bunker H lining the coast, I feel like that would be sufficient."

"We have the people, but supplies and rations are low," Crystal told her.

Plans were made, calculations figured out and set. Eventually, the plan was in place to fortify the coastal bunkers to the west, as well as the canyon gorge to the east.

A day and a half later, Paraffin and Ryder reached the edge of The Mosaic Forest. The edge of the forest was like looking through a waxy soap bubble. It was impossible to tell if the coast was clear through the protective force field. They waited for some time to try and tell if there was anyone or any activity on the other side. Even if there were someone on the other side, unless they knew the secrets of detection within The Mosaic Forest, the forest remained unseen and unnoticed. Another risk was that after permeating the cosmic force field protecting The Mosaic Forest, Ryder and Paraffin wouldn't be able to engage any of their cloaking apparatus for several minutes, making the importance of entering without detection imperative. Psychic abilities would also be rendered useless during this time.

Unfortunately, as soon as they penetrated the invisible plasma protecting The Mosaic Forest, the two travelers stepped directly in front of the path of an armed militant traveling on an ATV. To the armed bumpkin, it looked like the cosmic pair emerged from a mirage. The militant was none the wiser.

This hawkish individual, who went by the name Skeeter, was dressed in a brand-new starched dark green uniform, similar to that worn by Fidel Castro many centuries ago. He wore a thick leather belt that held his sidearm in a holster, pepper spray, handcuffs, zip ties, and a two-way walkie-talkie. Though he had perfect vision in both eyes, he wore an eyepatch because he thought it made him look tougher. Inside his soul, he was a sniveling, insecure coward and prejudice of anyone different than himself. On the outside, he behaved like a bully, following the lead of other hateful individuals that he fell in with. He believed wholeheartedly in The Queen's negative rhetoric, and was fueled by ignorance and hate. He was raised this way; his insecurities and fears wouldn't allow him to admit his own failures, faults, or insignificance. He wasn't part of The Queen's regiment, so he wasn't privy to any information The Queen may or may not have on the secrets of The Mosaic Forest. He was just an ignorant, self-righteous individual who was part of a self-appointed militia that kept themselves busy by stirring up hate and perpetuating a false narrative in order to do Queen Daffodil's evil bidding. Not able to admit his own faults and failings as a decent human being, he couldn't face his own insignificance. This fueled his misguided hatred and rage, turning it into a fireball/snowball effect, growing more and more intense because of his ego's need for constant reinforcement, supported by false feelings of superiority. Saddled with stupidity and lacking clear vision (due to only using one of his eyes to see, as well as no personal insight), the militiaman mistook Paraffin and Ryder for like-minded bigots.

Spitting black tobacco juice from his mouth before and after everything he said, the self-appointed lawman addressed the travelers.

"What ch'all doing on Pappy Wilson's property?"

He put his hand on the weapon in his holster and spit once more before following up with, "Y'all kin?"

Paraffin, quick to surmise the situation and in an unnoticed, slightly insulting tone, for which the bigot mistook as kinship, stated, "Beg-a-pardon?"

The militant spit and wiped his mouth with his grimy fingers. He repeated himself by asking, "What ch'all doing on Pappy Wilson's property? Y'all kin? If you ain't kin, you better git."

Skeeter started to reach for his long gun, which conveniently rested across the handlebars of his ATV.

"We ain't no kin. Wheeze da anti-Christ," Paraffin said, mockingly.

The militant didn't take kindly to sarcasm; and even though he wasn't a religious man, he took offense to the blasphemous nature of the ancient star traveler's comments. Paraffin expected to rile a response, but before the man could pull out his sidearm, Paraffin chuckled and said, "Of course I'm kin. Me and Lucas here are cousins on Elvira's side of the family."

"I don't know no Elvira," Skeeter replied.

Skeeter took notice of Ryder's transportation and inquired, "Say, what are you doing on a bicycle way out here in the middle of nowhere? What are you, anyway?"

"Now, don't you mind Lucas none, here," Paraffin said.

"I'll mind who I want and what I want, old man. Say, what are you? You some kind of al-bi-no?"

"No, I ain't no albino. Looky here, Mister…"

And with that, Paraffin held up his hand. With fingers stretched upwards and the palm of his hand pointing directly at the militant's face, he shot a beam of sound, hitting the rogue agent in the center of his forehead, just above his eyeballs. There wasn't a beam of light or a flash of any kind, no heat or laser – just a low, mid-range frequency that rendered the man helpless, leaving him in a state of physical and mental paralysis.

"When he comes to, he'll wake up wet and hungover, but he won't remember a thing. Let's get out of here."

Paraffin led Ryder on the far side of the ATV's tracks then backtracked from whence the bumpkin had come. They reached a creek that flowed into a tributary, which Paraffin knew would wind around to a canyon on the way to The Crystal City. Using one of the special features from the bicycle helmet, Ryder opened up a holographic map, and the two companions plotted their course.

"I think we should abandon our efforts in following the

tracks of the ATV. The tracks split off back at the creek. We need to follow this tributary. It'll lead us to The Crystal City, which is where The People's People movement resides. It's more of a home base. It's important we arrive quickly and safely. I don't expect them to track us, but in case they sense trouble and send their hounds to search for us, I'll de-scent our trail…but I doubt they'll even be on to us," Paraffin said.

CHAPTER NINETEEN

Skeeter woke up pissed off. And he had pissed himself. Disoriented and blurred vision – was it the humming in his head or was it the sound of Junior Jr. III's ATV that awoke him? Skeeter realized he was lying in the field next to his ATV with sopping wet trousers. Feeling the dampness that soaked through to his skin then smelling the urine on his fingers, Skeeter determined what happened.

"Oh, God. I pissed myself."

Skeeter's head was pounding, and he couldn't recollect what had become of himself. Junior Jr. III pulled up on his ATV surrounded by a pack of bloodhounds, mostly bitches. The hounds were riled up and they wouldn't stop screeching and howling no matter how much Junior Jr. yelled at them.

Skeeter and Junior Jr. III were second cousins, and Junior Jr. III was also his stepfather. Skeeter's dad and Junior Junior's dad were brothers, making them cousins. But after Skeeter's dad was killed in a barroom fight, Junior Jr. married Skeeter's mom. Making matters even weirder is that Junior Jr. was the one who killed Skeeter's pop. The killing was ruled as self-defense. Skeeter never held a grudge. He was known to say, "It's okay, Junior Jr. Daddy was drunk, and he was trying to keel you first."

Junior Jr. looked down at Skeeter, who wasn't quite ready to get up off the ground.

"What the hell happened to you?"

"Fuck if I know?"

"Why are your britches all wet on ya crotch and down yer leg?"

"Will you shut up, JJ? My head hurts," Skeeter said, rubbing his forehead where the beam of sound entered his skull.

Junior Jr. asked, "You sick? Want I to fetch Pappy? He'll get Doc Flotsam over here to look at cha."

"Gawd, no. Doc Flotsam ain't even fit to care for dead horses. Help me up, my legs are shaky."

"Man, you look to' up. You've been drinking already?"

"Not as much as to be as fucked up as this, I ain't. I tell ya, it's weird. I don't knows how I come out to be here or get this way."

"Maybe you getting the seizures like Mama had."

Skeeter fixated on the patterns of leaves on the ground

and said, "Twer'nt no seizure." Hints of annoyance were in his tone.

"Alright, Alriiiiiiight! Don't get snippy with me. I ain't trying to sass ya."

"I'm sorry, Junior Jr. I don't mean to be snippy."

"It's okay. Let's get you back home."

"Oh, Jeez-us H. Criminy," Skeeter paused, looked back and forth into the sky, and asked, "do you hear that?"

"Hear what?"

"That!"

Skeeter rubbed his forehead and moaned.

"That low humming sound. Where is it coming from? I think I'm gonna get sick."

Before Skeeter could say 'Look out,' his breakfast shot from his mouth and nose.

Junior Jr. chuckled and said, "Oh, boy. I bet you gonna feel better now."

"Shut erp!"

More breakfast and a little bit of fried varmint from the previous evening's dinner came up, too. After some hacking and coughing and blowing goop out, one nostril at a time, Skeeter felt a little better. The hounds started their incessant barking and howling once more.

"Can you ride?" Junior asked Skeeter.

The hounds began to howl even louder.

"Will you dogs be quiet? Shut it!"

In spite of Junior's commands, the hounds' ruckus wouldn't stop. The commotion, the sniffing, the howling – something was disturbing them.

"Something's got these bitches riled up. I wonder if something got you? These hounds seem awfully wound up 'bout something."

"Those damn dogs always cease to amaze me. They won't never quieten down."

"Yeah, they do, and they's for real more upset than usual this time."

"Let's get you home…then I want to see where these dogs take us."

"I don't need to go home. Let's just see if they's picks up on a scent. Oh, you can either look away or not. I known you seen it before."

Skeeter stripped off his commando pants and tied them over the hood of his ATV. His lily-white ass was bare for all to see.

"You gonna ride butt-ass naked?"

"I gotta dry the piss outta 'em. Come on, let's see if these bitches pick up anything."

Skeeter and Junior Jr., led by the bloodhounds crazed with an olfactory sensory overload, eventually found themselves at the fork in the road where the creek crossed the path to their homes. Their families lived in cabins forming a semi-circle in a compound, way up on a hill shaded by tall birch trees and surrounded by several small fields of crops. The bloodhounds, frantic with confusion, didn't lead them directly to the creek. The dogs ran in large, sweeping circles, sometimes circling the area more than three or four times before heading forward on the path. At the creek, they stopped for good, completely unsure of which direction to go.

"Hmph, whatever it was, they lost the scent."

"Those dogs are worthless."

Junior Jr. took offense to this. "Shut up!" he snapped. "These dogs led me to where you was at just now. If it weren't for them, you'd still be laying back there, wet in yer drawers."

"Aight, okay," Skeeter said, stepping down from his ATV. He put on his pants that had been drying on the hood. "Let's head up the creek or down the creek – either way, I don't care," he suggested.

"Hmm, come on, you worthless hounds. Which way should we go?" Junior Jr. asked. Put out with his beloved hounds, it was Junior Jr.'s turn to badmouth the dogs.

Some of the dogs milled about the creek, drinking the water; others were just standing in it, cooling off, admiring the scenery. The rest of the pack sat on the cool, damp bank licking themselves or scratching at a variety of itches, or snipping at pesky gnats flying about their snouts.

Rubbing his forehead, Skeeter shared his thoughts, "Well, if there was something out there, and if it or they went upstream, chances are they'd be found out by Pappy or the McAllister boys, who are up there running their clicit starvation pill mill. Whatever it was, if they went downstream, there's nothing really stopping them from going unnoticed."

Skeeter continued to rub his head and said, "Man, maybe I better go lay down. We don't even know what it is we're looking for or if there's anything for certain that had them dogs so riled up."

"Well, you go lay down a spell. I'm gonna take bitchy-bitch and one of the pups if they'll follow me, and head on down the creek a ways, just for the hell of it."

"Suit yourself. I'm beginning to wonder if you's right."

"Right about what?"

"Maybe I got the seizures like Mama had. Maybe they's weren't nothing else to it. There's might not be nothin' more to 'splain it."

"Oh, you probably et a bad varmint foot or you didn't git enough coffee in your mornin' liquor."

"This ain't liquor making me feel this way, JJ. I'm telling you, my head is throbbing so bad, it feels like something's about to pop right out of it."

"You go lay down. I'm-a walk down the creek a spell."

Junior Jr. III was from a long line of Juniors. His daddy, Junior Jr., and his daddy's daddy, Junior Sr., were all named after his great-granddaddy, Juniper. Eventually, the Juniper part was dropped, and they all went by Junior – every one of them. As a child, Junior Jr. III was the spitting image of his father, Junior Jr. Junior Number Three could walk into church or the store in town and old ladies would look at him and say, "My goodness, you must be Junior Jr.'s boy. You look just like him! And don't you look handsome in that suit!" or "shirt" or whatever they would say on that particular day.

CHAPTER TWENTY

The cosmic pair traveled at a leisurely pace. Ryder gently pedaled as Paraffin easily kept up, with his long strides that seemed to take no effort whatsoever.

"So, what's gonna happen to that fella back there?" Ryder asked.

They strolled through the woods, away from The Mosaic Forest and toward the great gorge leading them to the hidden Crystal City.

Paraffin chuckled. "Oh, he'll wake up with one doozy of a headache, but other than that…oh, and pissing himself, he'll be fine. He's lucky."

"How so?"

"I could've blasted him with a low subsonic frequency, causing him to poop in his pants, but I didn't. Other than feeling like he has the worst hangover of his life, he'll be okay. As long as he's not allergic."

"Allergic? To what, sound?"

"Well, yeah. Every so often, but very rarely, some reactions to the body can occur."

"Like what?"

"Like hives, a rash, or nausea; sometimes, people break out in acne or something kind of like the measles… and even in some cases…" Paraffin paused for a moment before continuing.

"In some cases, well, it's very rare; it's not very common, but in some cases, things happen. But it's extremely unlikely that something strange like that would pop up. I wouldn't worry about him. It's a very rare symptom that only on occasion causes unusual things to happen. But only in the most extreme cases."

Paraffin paused again, searching for the right words.

"Causes *what*?" Ryder stopped pedaling, putting both feet on the ground and straddling the bike.

"Well," Paraffin looked up at the clouds passing by. "Reactions. People have reactions..."

Changing the subject, he said, "Hey, I'm getting hungry. Should we forage the forest flora for something to eat?"

Ryder agreed, and with little effort, the pair rustled up a few handfuls of mushrooms and truffles, along with some herbs and berries. They sat in a quiet location, surrounded by the old-growth forest – a few of the lone survivors of the recent destruction – and enjoyed their lunch. This solitary patch of ancient, woody giants survived years of war, pollution, and climate change. Each in their own thoughts, the noble travelers munched in silence on the delectables they found from rummaging through the forest floor.

Ryder's train of thought broke. Both their eyes met. They each smiled with mouthfuls of food, giggling and choking as they began to laugh.

"I guess I was hungrier than I thought," Ryder said.

Paraffin nodded and added, "Me too. I'm feeling much better. I was starting to get a little run down."

"Being from another planet, was it weird eating and getting used to food here on Earth? How is it that the nutrition we get from food works the same way for you?"

"Well, it was a gradual process to assimilate into taking in nutrition here on Earth. Our ships were well fortified with our own supplies, but eventually, our people had to adjust to the food sources on this planet. For me, being born from a petri dish, I was easily adaptable. Many of our astronauts didn't adapt, and most of our people didn't survive the transition."

"How many of you are there?"

"Hard to say. Not many compared to the vast number that originally entered into this galaxy. Some have adapted and metamorphosed well enough to live and mate here on Earth."

A contemplative hush fell over the forest as the two continued gnawing on mushrooms, truffles, and plants.

"Paraffin?" Ryder spoke with a childlike innocence. "Why can't people get along? Why must so many people hate, fight, and kill one another? How did everyone's beliefs get so far out of whack that they stopped thinking of others as fellow human beings? Doesn't everyone, no matter their race, color, or creed, deserve equal kindness and understanding? Why must people impose their own beliefs on others?"

"Sometimes…oftentimes, it's been people's greed, or they were just raised to hate," Paraffin answered. "Greed and hatred that makes it okay to kill and steal from one another, especially if those people are different than you. When people judge others by how they look – when people don't look like *they* do – they don't see them as equals. People, over time, kill what they don't know or understand. Ignorance and free will are a dangerous combination. They want to destroy what they perceive as threats. Often, it threatens their own fragile egos or their insatiable need to control others. At times, it's religious biases or bigotry…or for any number of misguided reasons."

Ryder nodded and stated, "There was a lot of fighting in my family when I was growing up. Like most people, we were poor and didn't have enough to eat and couldn't even afford government-issued starvation pills. Every month, my parents blamed each other. They screamed and yelled and sometimes, things got violent. When I was a kid, they'd fight and argue all the time. Even as a child, I couldn't understand why they couldn't just get along. It was scary and I couldn't take it, so I ran away. I was able to take care of myself just fine, and I think I turned out okay. I just wish people wouldn't fuss and fight."

Paraffin replied, "My planet's people didn't have those issues. We're a much older species. There was a time, many millennia ago, that our planet had the strife and growing pains that Earth has, but we evolved. Greed, corruption, slavery, bigotry, wars, even religious conflicts…we evolved beyond all of that. Religious wars and conflicts of ideology were resolved when our species learned to recognize the good in all philosophies, and accepted science and spirituality as one. We learned to accept others with differences of opinion. We alleviated hate, we learned to love, and we accept others for who they are. We treat each other with the same kindness and respect that we'd want to be treated with. And we stopped trying to force everyone to worship and believe the same ideology."

"How hard is that?" Ryder asked.

Not waiting for an answer, Ryder said, "Pretty difficult, I guess. Nearly impossible for many."

"On my planet, things didn't get as bad as it is here, but I feel like you Earthlings can still make the changes you need to save this planet and your species."

Ryder saw the good in Paraffin's soul, and it became clear just how good of a soul his was. So much so, that Ryder abruptly changed the subject by asking, "Did you ever have a soulmate or a spouse? Do you still have loved ones here on Earth?"

A look of anguish washed over Paraffin's face. After a long pause, he sighed and explained, "I fell in love once. She was a lovely human being, and I know that she was very interested in me, too. She was so kind, and her hair smelled like flowers. But I knew that I would outlive her by many generations. I couldn't bear the thought of losing her, so I never pursued the love of my life…for which I now regret. I didn't realize that the pain of living this long without having known that joy, the regret of not pursuing that love, would be far greater than having that love for one extended moment in time and then never having it again. I made the decision out of fear, and now I suffer."

Ryder felt the pain and sorrow as Paraffin spoke.

Paraffin went on to say, "So, I threw myself into my work for many centuries…developing the science, along with the technology created by Noah Billingsworth, that's going to hopefully save this beautiful, godforsaken rock."

"How long ago was this lost love? What was her name?"

"Her name?" Paraffin's face lit up with a smile, a sparkle twinkled in his eyes. Paraffin took a deep breath and let it out slowly.

"Her name," he said, softly, "was Cleopatra."

"What?! The great queen of Egypt?"

"Oh, heavens no! Different Cleopatra, but this girl was awesome. I should've married her and made her *my* queen. Let that be a lesson to you, Ryder. Follow your heart and your gut. Always trust your instincts."

"My instincts are telling me we should get out of here."

"I agree. I'm feeling it, too."

No sooner was it said, the sound of a twig snapping underfoot could be heard. Paraffin motioned to be quiet.

The pair gathered their meager belongings and ventured toward the high ground. Soon, they heard the unison sound of boots marching instep as a battalion of troops gathered below them. Procuring a safe vantage point, hidden behind a large boulder blanketed with scrub brush, Ryder and Paraffin looked on as a medium-sized brigade casually marched through the area where only moments earlier, they were picnicking and pontificating about life. Their tensions and fears subsided while they surmised the situation. The soldiers appeared to be taking their duties lightly, as evidenced by their laughter and good-natured ribbing.

CHAPTER TWENTY-ONE

After searching the creek and other small confluences, Junior Jr. hiked back to the compound where Skeeter laid on his mattress in a disruptive sleep. He tossed and turned, haunted with fever dreams as the agony in his head persisted. Junior peeked into Skeeter's room to see if he was okay. Skeeter, unable to sleep, was awake. He was standing and staring before the mirror on his mama's vanity, looking at himself and gently touching his forehead.

"How are you doing?"

"Not so good. Look at this – I got a big ol' bump on my head."

"Mmm hmm, that's what it is, alright. And I bet that's what happened. Somehow, you fell off your ATV and whacked your noggin'. I bet ya probably give yerself a cun-cussion."

"Man, the way this thing hurts and the way it's throbbing…" Skeeter paused. He looked back in the mirror, gently touching the sore spot between his eyes. He continued, "It's almost like it's alive, growing out of me like a giant zit."

Junior Jr. tried reassuring Skeeter, "Man, you just cracked your skull. You're okay. Remember when cousin Wanna popped his head fallin' outta that tree?"

Skeeter didn't let him finish. "Yeah, but the knot on Wanna's head popped out instantly; this thing is just now showing up."

"Yeah, that's weird, alright."

As the night went on, the growth on Skeeter's forehead continued to grow. Tears rolled down his cheeks when a round mass broke through the skin like a giant blister. Once the massive growth broke through the skin, the agonizing pain broke, too. Now, his forehead felt thick, his mind confused.

Over the course of the evening, the mass kept growing, eventually protruding far enough that Skeeter no longer needed a mirror to see it. Starting out with a thick, wide base the mass eventually tapered down to a fine point at the tip. It twisted slowly, reminiscent of an ancient vine forming into a perfect cone that hardened like a bone. The shaft jetted out of Skeeter's forehead.

Junior Jr. wanted to touch it.

"Get away from it, Junior! This damn thing's making me cross-eyed, but I can still see you wanting to reach out and touch it."

"It's like you growed an antler, only it's out of your forehead."

Both men walked over and peered into the mirror together.

Junior Jr. said, "It's like a single antler. You got you one horn – a uni-horn. Oh my God, Skeeter, you're turning into a unicorn! Let me look at your feet. Do you got hooves?"

Junior Jr. grabbed Skeeter's hands.

"Let me look at your fingers. No, they're not turning into hooves. I guess you're okay."

"Dammit, Junior Jr.! I'm not okay!"

CHAPTER TWENTY-TWO

Freshening up with water and rations, the soldiers decided to take a long break and rest. They stopped at the exact spot under the same trees where Ryder and Paraffin had previously lounged. Ryder and Paraffin traveled lightly to and from their previous resting place, so none of the sentry would notice any traces they may have left behind. The grade up the hill where they hid was very steep, giving them some assurance that the soldiers wouldn't care to exert themselves enough to make the effort to climb up the hill to search the area. The duo stayed motionless and quiet, being careful not to draw any attention to themselves. They knew if they needed to engage their cloaking devices, they could. But they were hoping it wouldn't come to that.

They could hear the soldiers laughing and bragging about sexual exploits, troubles with wives, general boasting, and/or complaining. The men sounded lazy and in no hurry to continue their task for The Queen. It seemed as though their break would never end. Finally, the captain called everyone to order, and the soldiers began to line up, performing an about-face back in the direction of the palace.

Paraffin and Ryder had almost drifted off into a light sleep while waiting for the battalion's break to end. Paraffin awoke with a cramp in his lower body. Stretching out, his foot dislodged a small rock, sending a tiny boulder and many small pebbles racing down the hill. The captain screamed, ordering the men to take cover. After a quick study of the situation, he sent a portion of his troops up the embankment while the majority stayed back to give cover if needed.

Scrambling to get afoot, Ryder wasn't able to engage the cloaking device on the helmet or bicycle. Paraffin, however, was able to stand up, his long frame erect and balanced, and quickly disappeared from sight as he vanished into the fabric of his surroundings.

Ryder struggled to propel the bike forward, making little progress up the steep slope. The weapons on the bike jammed and wouldn't fire. All efforts failed. Ryder was overpowered, captured, bound, and carted off to The Queen's tower. Removing the chain from the bike, the soldiers used it to bind Ryder's hands before throwing the captive into a cage fastened out of cedar and oak branches. The cage was transported on a primitive one-axle cart. The journey back to the kingdom was an arduous affair. Ryder kept flopping around from the uneven towing of the guards pulling the cart over the bumpy terrain. Ryder's main concern was the bicycle, keeping it in sight as it lay discarded on the side of the trail.

"You can't take me and leave my bike. Seriously, don't leave my bike. Just kill me."

"Oh, killing's too good for you. The Queen will have her way with you and then you'll wish you were dead."

The menacing glare on the captain's face lit up with joy when he spoke of The Queen's evil. He took pleasure in imagining the torture and trauma The Queen would inflict on this wretched urchin.

Not wanting to appear weak or scared, Ryder hid the fears and tears, beginning to weep silently. Ryder hadn't thought of the loss of the entire family since the final takeover of their city. Mother, father, all the brothers and sisters, aunts and uncles, and beloved grandparents. Now, with the dismantling and loss of the bike, it was as if all those suppressed feelings and the sadness of loss was as fresh as the day death stared back from each of their faces.

Suddenly, a seven-foot-long beam of light hovered above the ground directly in front of the sentry's path. The soldiers drew forth their weapons and stood at the ready. The shimmering beam of light parted and opened up into an oval, resembling a giant womb. As it opened, out from it stepped the translucent celestial being, Paraffin. He was glowing in a golden aura. Dropping their weapons to shield their eyes from the spectacular rays of light shooting out of every pore in Paraffin's body, the squinting soldiers were forced to look away. Ryder didn't need to squint or look away; the warm, golden glow was comforting. The bicycle chain cutting into Ryder's wrists fell to the ground as the golden light covered the entire meadow. The cuts and blood on Ryder's wrists began to heal, just like droplets of evaporating water.

The troop captain, decorated in medals for mind control, resisted the powers of the golden light longer than the other soldiers. Clinching a revolver, he stiffly lifted his arm, attempting to control his trembling limb. As much as he tried, he could not muster the strength to pull the trigger. Many of the soldiers fell to the ground, crying and rolling around in agony, some curling up into fetal positions. Others began to frolic about, as if clumsy ballerinas had entered their bodies.

"What is this? Who are you?" the bewildered captain asked.

"Who I am and what this is is pretty much what it is. I'm a celestial being trapped here by fate. While here on your planet, I have now learned my kismet and purpose. Perhaps my destiny's purpose is to pass on what I've learned from the knowledge of my own planet's suffering. We had similar issues eons before I existed. But on my planet, we learned to evolve and survive in spite of these catastrophes," Paraffin answered.

Stuck in a momentary paralysis, the officer's helplessness rendered him complacent. All he could say was, "I don't get it."

Paraffin explained, "You don't stop hate with hate. You

can't end war with wars. What has Queen Daffodil ever done for you? Or for anybody? Why do you take pleasure in presiding over the pain and misery of others? What is wrong with the golden rule that exists with every intelligent life force in every vast universe? 'Treat each other as you'd want to be treated.' That saying existed long before Jesus Christ walked the Earth dozens of centuries ago. It existed in civilizations across the many galaxies and beyond this plane of existence zillions and zillions of light-years ago. One of the great Native American tribes, the Shawnee, who lived on this very land several hundred years ago, had a saying: 'We are all one child spinning through Mother Sky.' What incredible insight! That has always been and is still true."

Finally able to break free from the cosmic paralysis of Paraffin's golden glow, the officer in charge was able to speak, "I'm going to lie down. My body feels rubbery."

And with that, he curled up for a nap, bunching up a handful of leaves to serve as a pillow. Ryder was impressed.

"Wow, he's already snoring," Ryder noted.

"Purring like a little kitten," Paraffin said.

"Come on, let's get out of here."

"I'm afraid this is where our travels together part," Paraffin explained. "I'm going to wait for the squad to recover from the sensory overload I've given them. I don't want them to follow you to The Crystal City. I'll stay behind and try to persuade them to change their perspective. This is kind of a large group for me to sway into a different belief system, but if I can continue reprogramming them, it will be beneficial to the cause. We could use their help in rebuilding the structures of the damaged regions. My plan is to catch back up with you just before you transverse the gorge leading to The Crystal City."

Using his long appendages, Paraffin drew a map in the dirt as he gave specific directions to the route Ryder was to take. After all the instructions were made clear, Paraffin walked back to the oval beam of light still hovering above the ground. Using both hands, he separated the light, opening it and reaching far inside. He extracted Ryder's bike, equipped with a new chain and sparkling as if it had been freshly waxed.

"Wow, it's beautiful!" Ryder exclaimed. Grateful, as if Paraffin had returned all the family members and loved ones taken so long ago.

Paraffin then offered one more piece of instruction. "If we don't meet up before you reach the foothills of the gorge, you must continue on without me. You'll travel deep into this gorge then scale the cliff onto the other side to find The Crystal City. You will meet a shaman along the way. Some call him a witchdoctor, while others call him a medicine man. He is all these things. He'll grant you safe passage, and he has the wisdom and the skills to assist you. Without his guidance, you may still find The Crystal City, but there's a greater chance you will perish without his help. The shaman will also be part of the cosmic equation to send the psychic message to Mars."

CHAPTER TWENTY-THREE

Back at The Crystal City, The People's People continued to implement their experiments. The tests and lab results were more favorable than anticipated, and the signs of healthy progress were advancing quicker than expected. Spirits were high. The results across the mountains and into the prairies were favorable, yet several of the top scientists on Crystal's team were despondent when they arrived for the mid-morning meeting. There was further evidence that reversing the detrimental direction in the Earth's environment, which had occurred over centuries of abuse, could not be altered at this point.

"So, what's up?" Crystal asked. "Why are our efforts not enough?"

The lead scientist explained, "Even at the pace we're currently on for Earth's recovery, even if we keep the pace we're on, with no more environmental setbacks or wars, distractions, or catastrophes, even if we didn't have to contend with the evil forces of Queen Daffodil and all those enforcing her evil and corrupt biddings, we may not recover quickly enough before our ecosystem sucks all the remaining oxygen we have left out of the planet."

"That's right," the second specialist added. "It'll be like a domino effect – a lightning-speed ripple that will turn our planet into dust and ash, occurring as quickly as a breeze blowing across a field of wheat."

"What can we do? What should we do?" Crystal and Grace asked, one following the other.

Both men were silent and peered at each other, hoping the other one would speak first.

Finally, the scientist spoke up. "Well—"

"We have an intuitive that we've been working with," the specialist interrupted.

"That's right. Besides all the scientific data that we've accumulated, we're also working with…"

"…a psychic!"

"I'd call her more of an intuitive."

"Psychic, intuitive, paranormal, whatever! We're using the help."

"The skills…"

"…of a…"

"…clairvoyant!" they announce in unison.

"Her name is Claire the Clairvoyant," said the specialist, with a touch of pride.

"Well, that's fantastic. Neither I nor Grace have a problem with that. Whatever it takes to save our planet and the existence of mankind. So, what does Claire the Clairvoyant think?"

"They're getting a strong sense that there's help on the way. They've picked up strong readings at Franklin's Tower that some sort of cosmic occurrence has been in play for quite some time, but…" the lead scientist stopped.

"But what?" Crystal asked.

"But Claire isn't sure who this person is or what the missing link might be."

The specialist picked up the explanation. "Yes, she doesn't know and doesn't think that the person traveling to us is the only missing link."

"That's right. They think that they're perhaps part of the solution, but not the total equation, as it were."

"Okay then, what do we do in the meantime?"

"Keep doing what you're already doing. Have your team continue implementing their experiments. The results have been favorable, and the positive effects are beginning to show."

"In the meantime, we hope Queen Daffodil slows down with her senseless destruction. We hope she continues to fail in her attempts of locating the capital or any of the other main outposts or command centers."

Even though greener, cleaner environments were beginning to grow, spreading from The Crystal City far and wide to the fields and mountains, over prairies and forests, there were still cities in the countryside that were barren and filthy, with polluted water and dry dust for dirt where grass and plants no longer grew. The dirt of the dead fields wafted into the air with every wind or any passersby, stirring up dust particles, adding to the already-polluted air that was choking with chemicals and gas. Parts of the Earth were recovering, while others were falling apart.

Crystal and Grace, along with their top leaders and a team of scientists led by specialists Norman and Orville Poff, continued to follow the guidance of Claire the Clairvoyant. Claire and the scientists developed a psychic energy-seeking radar screen that they could use in their attempts to track the location of the unknown traveler headed their way. The screen picked up many energy sources, but Claire and the team of scientists used deductive reasoning to determine which energy source actually was the anointed messenger.

Claire closed her eyes and slipped into a trance.

She stated, "It's imperative that this messenger find the shaman, Elizer. Elizer means 'the help of my God'. Without the help of the shaman, I do not see the messenger surviving or getting through to us."

"Should we form a search team and look for this traveler?" Grace asked.

"No. No, we shouldn't."

With eyes closed, Claire watched a scenario play out on the other side of her eyelids, inside her mind.

"We need to wait here. The more of us here in one spot focusing on bringing that person to us creates an attractive force, just like the gravitational pull of a magnet. A collective energy will help draw this person here to us, provided they don't get intercepted by enemy forces or any of the militant renegades scavenging and wreaking havoc on their own," she directed.

But this messenger…what happens if they don't find the shaman? How will they find this shaman?" Grace asked emphatically.

Claire's eyes popped wide open, as if jolted out of a deep sleep. She said, "There is a problem. My vision tells me the witchdoctor may be sick and dying. It's possible he's already deceased."

"Who told you this?" Grace wanted to know.

"One of the voices in my vision spoke to me. The sensations were strong. The shaman, Elizer, is near death and has possibly already succumbed to injuries from the sword either figuratively or literally, I can't tell. I'm trying not to worry. I'm trying to stay focused on the positive, but there's a chance our kismet is foretold."

CHAPTER TWENTY-FOUR

Ryder felt despondent after leaving Paraffin with the sleepy soldiers back in the woods. A sense of melancholy that could only be relieved by one thing: the rapid force of pedaling with all one's might. A spirited determination that could send a person into a trance, detaching them from time and space. Effort became nonexistent. Ryder flowed through untraveled paths, floating past trees and rocks and other obstacles with the grace of a cosmic skier hitting the slaloms of space and time with a hypnotic ease, carefree, never once venturing into danger. The slightest error in movement would've easily resulted in a bone-breaking injury or possibly death.

After what seemed like mere moments, but actually equated to several hours, Ryder road into the darkness, transversing the night and the forest, eventually reaching the edge of a mesa. The vast darkness turned to purple then blues and yellows as the morning sunshine started to rise. As the darkness turned to light, Ryder saw a stream far in the distance. The water was clear, and there was a shimmer of the river rocks making up its bed.

Sensing no danger, but feeling like someone was watching, Ryder turned to see the face of an angelic native princess. She was perfectly unkempt, with dark tufts of hair flowing over her bare shoulders. Her essence radiated. The morning sunshine seemed to beam from her being.

"Are you the shaman?" Ryder asked.

"No, but he's been expecting you. I'm Nora, daughter of Elizer."

Nora led Ryder through several mounds of earth. Each mound was covered in grass and moss. The path became a labyrinth of twists and turns through a series of these mounds. The deeper into the labyrinth, the higher the walls became until it was unclear to Ryder if they were venturing underground. The mountains shaded the morning light, losing the feeling of daytime. After a journey several miles into the maze of earth and growth, Nora pulled back a woven shield of ivy leading into a round kiva lit by the glow of a small fire, which was mostly reduced to embers. Several candles made from beeswax and a lantern lit by the blubber of a large mammal also provided light.

"My father is very ill. I don't think he can heal himself

this time. He has cured himself over many tides. Centuries worth of tides rolling in and out with the seduction of the moon. I'm his youngest child, fathered by a man nearly 370 years old," Nora explained.

"That's astonishing," Ryder replied.

"My father has had many wives. My mom was a young woman when they met, but Elizer was over 300 years her elder."

"Where is she now?"

"Unfortunately, she was killed, like so many others, by the hands of Queen Daffodil. Now, my ancient father, wounded badly in a battle he refused to fight, maintained his beliefs as a pacifist and will soon make his transition."

Looking around the curved walls of the kiva, Ryder's eyes adjusted to the dim light inside the hut. Ryder noticed the sparseness of objects in the room. The flickering light speckled across the hut, casting shadows that moved across the clay floor and walls. The silhouette of a chair danced with the table in a tango of shadows to the music of the flames. The wind howled through the foothills leading to the gorge. Ryder homed in on the single bedframe holding the elder shaman, Elizer, who was swaddled in a layer of blankets tucked into a cocoon.

"He'll wake soon. Would you like some breakfast?"

Ryder hadn't eaten since parting ways with Paraffin. Just the mention of food made the pangs of hunger intensify. Nora bent over the coals and stirred the fire. Using a hook attached to a wooden handle, she removed the lid of a cast iron skillet. Inside were steaming layers of dough made from a thick cornmeal polenta. Gingerly picking one out of the pan, she placed it on a plate and covered it with stewed beans and grits. She poured diced tomato purée sauce with peppers, garlic, and clove onto the plate then handed it to Ryder. She served herself a plate, but by the time she did, Ryder had consumed every last morsel.

After breakfast, Elizer began to slowly stir. He cleared his throat and sat up from underneath the tightly fitting covers, like Gulliver breaking free from the ropes of his tiny captors on the beach in the fabled tale. The wool covers fell from his shoulders.

Elizer turned and locked eyes with Ryder. He said, "We've been expecting you."

When their eyes met, Ryder saw the old soul of a young man, but noticed the rest of his body – the frail, old man who remained. So old and frail, he could barely lift himself out of bed. It was apparent that this person was not going to be able to lead Ryder on the final part of the journey. The most difficult and treacherous part still lay ahead.

Standing in silence, Ryder's mind raced with a million questions. Fixated on nothing, Elizer stared at the ground. After several deep inhalations and exhales, the medicine man looked up at Ryder as he spoke.

"What is your name, heavenly star child?"

Ryder was stunned by his words and said nothing.

"What do they call you?"

"My name is Ryder."

Elizer grinned and said, "Ryder…that's good. So, you're like the Greek god, Hermes."

"Who?"

"Hermes, the offspring of Zeus and Maia. He was the fastest of all the gods. I see you have the same bone structure," Elizer pointed to Ryder's face and continued, "up here in the cheeks and your chin."

Elizer made a face, puckered his lips, and stuck out his chin. The shaman cleared his throat, but it turned into a series of coughing and hacking up phlegm. Nora brought a small pan and a cool rag over to him. Elizer spat into the pan as she gently wiped the damp towel across her father's forehead.

With his lungs now cleared, Elizer said, "Ryder, as you can see, I'm not well. I'm an old man. I cannot go with you on your journey, but what I can do is give you a vision. I can guide you into a trance – a trance that will enable you to witness your possible outcome. An outcome chosen for you by fate. Your vision will show you the answers that you need. You will be given the path you must take; however, if you don't recognize the answers in your vision, if you can't decipher the code or the information given to you, all of this, it will do you no good. But, if you are the chosen one who is on the right spiritual path, the light will come to you and the knowledge you need will be yours. Trust your instincts and listen to the whispers of the universe."

"How does this work? I mean, the trance. How do you guide me through a trance?" Ryder inquired.

"Nora is going to prepare a special spirit tea. It's made from medicinal plants and mushrooms that will evoke the spirits into your vision. The gods will have you by the hand

and you can relax and go wherever it takes you. I'll be right here with you. If it ever gets to be frightening or too much, I will guide you through it."

Nora brought out a wicker tray with tiny cups of china and a small porcelain kettle with matching painted designs. She carefully poured steaming hot tea into the cups. After a few moments of drinking the tea, Ryder began noticing the breath and how satisfying each inhalation was.

Soon, the vision started.

Ryder's mother and father were standing, facing one another. Sadness, the loss – it was almost more than one could bear. Another deep inhale and exhale, and a feeling of comfort and calm came over Ryder. Another deep breath, and something happened. Something Ryder had never experienced before: the overwhelming reassurance that things were okay. At this very moment, right now, everything felt protected and safe. It felt as though everything was going to be okay.

No longer looking at mom and dad, Ryder was now soaring through the sky with the ease and vision of an eagle. Flying high above some cliffs, an old-growth forest towered next to the ocean. Deep blue waters crashed against the cliff, tossing logs the size of freight cars about like matchsticks. Ryder could feel the rush of the wind. Wings flapping, gliding, turning, soaring about, dipping into the trees, through the branches, landing on a trail. No longer flying, but walking with the legs of a human, Ryder could hear voices and sensed that danger was near.

The road branched off into several choices, yet one path

was lit with a green glow. Ryder walked through a drapery of vines before slipping and falling through a shaft, eventually landing in a cave illuminated by crystals. Struggling to stay awake, Ryder decided to lie down, soon falling into a deep, deep sleep. Dreaming inside a dream, witnessing ancient ancestors, each farther back in time, with every passing moment of the dream, Ryder traveled through multiple generations of ancestors, each dream going back farther and farther, and deeper and deeper until it was so far back in time, the ancestors weren't standing upright. Instead, they were reptiles and tadpoles and tiny amoebas, all floating around in pond scum. And these were ancestors, too.

Time started spinning forward. There was the sound of a distant drum, a single drum, accompanied by a simple gourd shaker, with only a few seeds inside of it. Voices, sometimes three or four of them, chanted in a unified call-and-response. The sounds reminded Ryder that within oneself is a soul; and Ryder's soul was tied into those chants, the drum, and the gourd rattle.

Ryder's eyes opened. Looking back was the face of Nora, perfectly unkempt, holding a burning stick of sage. Seeing the face of God in the swirling pattern of smoke coming off the embers of burning sage, Ryder was alive once more.

Elizer was the one chanting and shaking the gourd maraca. Another medicine man named Afonja was playing a small drum. He held the drum in one hand, under his arm, and used a mallet elaborately carved out of redwood with a soft leather ball tied around the end of the stick to strike the membrane of the little wooden drum.

Nora, resting on her knees, leaned forward and gently placed her fingers on Ryder's chest. She continued leaning in and softly kissed Ryder's mouth. As they kissed, it was as if air and water filled the empty soul. Her touch was like electricity coursing through the skin. Their veins pulsated in unison. Glowing beams of love shone forth and filled the forest air.

Ryder felt purpose.

Elizer and Afonja stopped their chant and song. The kiva was quiet. Everyone seemed to awaken at the same time. With their eyes now opened, people smiled and nodded at each other in agreement.

Elizer softly spoke. "Your dreams, your vision, your sadness, your grief, your happiness – those belong to you. Be proud of it, own it. Nobody can take any of that away from you. Your sufferings, your triumphs, your fears, your conquering of your fears, your ability to overcome…that is yours. That belongs to you, and you deserve it. The Eagle has guided you, led you here, to your chosen path. Your journey has been a lifetime in the making, but it has just now begun. When you get there, you will know what to do. Trust in yourself and you will know what to do. You'll make the right choice." He paused, closing his eyes, and taking several deep breaths as he slowly rocked back and forth.

Opening his eyes, he said, "I cannot go with you. My body will not allow it. But my mind and soul will be with you. I will hold my vision..."

He closed his eyes and took in another deep breath before finishing his thought, "…for you to be safe wherever you need to be."

He pointed to his forehead, right between his eyes, and said, "I will keep my eagle eye out for you. You cannot be unsafe if the eagle eye sees you through."

Elizer paused once again, taking in another contemplative breath, and stated, "I cannot go with you, but Nora can. She will lead you. She knows the forest and can guide you through a safe passage. I know from my visions that certain people need to be brought together to make the magic of the grand experiment successful. Nora possesses the same personal chemical body equation and personal periodic number to make the magic happen."

Surprised and bewildered, Nora's eyes widened. She smiled and shook her head. "Are you sure, father? Why not one of the others? Abraham's son, Zimran, is a warrior and is known for his strength—"

Elizer held up a frail hand and waved her off as he tried not to cough. Once he regained his composure and caught his breath, he further explained, "No, child. We don't need a warrior or a fighter; we need a person with vision. We need the type of warrior that you are, a person with knowledge. Knowledge is power. We need someone with grace and the know-how that you have. Someone who can glide through the forest unnoticed and undisturbed. Someone who understands nature, both the seen and the unseen. And most importantly of all, you have the same DNA and cosmic fingerprint as me. You have the same cosmic equation needed to send the telepathic psychic message through to Mars. Use your instincts, and your knowledge will take you there. You're the shaman now, Nora, my love. You are the divine spirit – the chosen one from this tribe."

Elizer started coughing up phlegm as he tried to catch his breath. Afonja gave him a ladle of water. Nora bent over to kiss her father. She covered him with the wool blankets and tucked him in for what turned out to be his eternal sleep.

CHAPTER TWENTY-FIVE

Paraffin kept a careful watch over the soldiers. One by one, they awoke from their cosmic slumber. By the time the last of the battery came to, it didn't take much persuading to get the soldiers to agree with his reasoning. They had seen enough of Queen Daffodil's evil and greed to realize that there was nothing good in it for them. They needed little encouragement to overcome their fears and follow through with what they knew was the right thing to do. Plus, they had witnessed enough of what they would call 'His magic' (referring to Paraffin) to be convinced to stop following the orders of Queen Daffodil. Paraffin and the troops were now en route to one of the secret entrances of Queen Daffodil's underground lair. Her subterranean palace fortress expanded far and wide below the Earth's surface. The mining to build her underground city triggered the volcanoes to erupt, destroying Yellowstone National Forest. The destructive forces were close to annihilating the planet's entire population, bringing humanity to the brink of extinction. Paraffin felt certain that if he could penetrate into Queen Daffodil's hidden kingdom, he could plant the seeds of thought and reason into more of her soldiers. The idea of change was possible. Still, he knew his mind powers alone weren't enough to conquer an entire kingdom, but if he convinced even one person or a small group of individuals at a time, he could spread the idea of change, love, and understanding. Peace was possible.

The troops came to a halt when word came back from a scout that some unidentified militants on ATVs were approaching from the southeast coordinate.

"What do you see, Corporal? How many are there?" the captain asked, obviously concerned.

"Sir, there's approximately eight or nine ATVs driven by unknown individuals, most of whom are wearing hunting outfits and army surplus uniforms with no insignia to indicate what group they're affiliated with."

"Alright. Nice work, Corporal. Everyone, arm your weapons, but do *not* engage the enemy or fire upon them without my declaration," the captain ordered.

Paraffin felt his pervasive grip loosening on the soldiers. He had managed to subdue and influence them one or two at a time; the entirety of a small group could be persuaded more easily than a larger group. However, if the soldiers fell back into their aggressive posturing, all of his positive influence would amount to nothing.

"Woah, hold on a minute. I thought we all agreed that you can't stop war with war, violence with violence, hatred with hatred," Paraffin said.

"Sir, this may be true, but there's a lot of forces out here that still want to do others harm. Until a paradigm shift happens everywhere, we have to prepare ourselves for contrary opinions and mindsets, some of which may turn violent. These self-armed militant wackos are even more unpredictable and dangerous than most of The Queen's forces."

"Well, I don't know about that, but if there's less than a dozen of them, please don't open fire on them. I can manifest a change of heart in them as long as they're bright enough to have a mind to influence. There *are* some creatures, not many, but some, whose minds can't be changed...not when they don't have a mind to change."

As the militants on the ATVs approached, Paraffin noticed the person leading the pack. This particular militant stood out, and the other soldiers also noticed it – a long horn growing out of the forehead of Junior Jr.'s cousin, Skeeter. The captain overheard Paraffin mumbling.

"I'm sorry what did you say?"

"Oh, well, I…um…I said poor fellow, looks like he was allergic. That's so unusual."

"Allergic? To what?"

"Hmm? Oh, allergic to sound. A beam of sound. I've run

across this fellow once before and rendered him helpless and unconscious with a beam of sound."

Paraffin pointed to the middle of his forehead.

"I hit him right here, right in the middle of his third eye, and up his forehead into his crown chakra. I didn't mean to hurt him, but once every blue ox, it'll happen."

"What will?"

"An allergic reaction. That's why the skinny one in front has the horn growing out of his forehead."

Paraffin diverted his attention from the captain by smiling and waving to the approaching militants.

"Hi, hello. How's it going?" Every greeting was aimed with a nod, each time to a different militant. Paraffin gave an extra smile and nod to Junior Jr. and Skeeter.

"I'm sorry. Looks like you were allergic after all."

"Excuse me, sir," Skeeter replied.

Paraffin nodded his head and pointed with his nose toward Skeeter's new addition.

"There, looks like you were allergic. The horn – it wasn't intentional. It's a very uncommon side effect."

"Do I know you?" Skeeter asked.

The clicking of guns cocking and chambers being prepared reverberated in the stillness of the woods. The tension was palpable. Paraffin radiated golden light and raised both hands, palms facing toward the militants and their ATVs, flooding them with a pure illustrious frequency. He shone a light that reverberated through their bones. The militant posse began to feel safe and comfortable, as if being inside a mother's womb. Some of them began weeping, while others grew angry and disoriented trying to fire their weapons, but none of them worked. The weapons either misfired or jammed. Paraffin started feeling lightheaded and nauseous. He knew he wouldn't be able to continue with this level of energy without recharging his body for several hours. He was going to need to reason logically with the militants. He hoped that the soldiers didn't return to using forces of brutality in trying to solve the situation.

Skeeter struggled to keep his focus. He asked the slender, opaque being the same question as earlier.

"Do I know you, mister…" he said, looking Paraffin up and down before adding, "whatever you are?"

Junior Jr. joined in. "Yeah, what are you?"

Paraffin felt his psychic strength weakening and decided to be blunt with his answer. He explained, "I'm a celestial being from a different dimension. I was born in a petri dish on a spacecraft several thousand years ago. Our fleet was sucked into your galaxy in kind of a space hiccup. I've watched your entire species over thousands of years, and I've now discovered that it's my great destiny to try and help you evolve. Oh…and I'm sorry about the horn."

"Wait a minute, *you* did this?" Skeeter stroked his horn.

Junior Jr. piped up and asked, "Hold on, you're a spaceman?"

"Essentially, we all are," Paraffin answered.

"When did you…what do you know about this horn?"

"I zapped you with a sound wave a few days ago to keep you from stopping me and someone I was traveling with. I was helping them. We're on an important mission to help save your planet."

"Hey, Skeeter, I think we should kill it," Junior Jr. said.

"Shoot it, shoot it!" the other hillbillies hollered.

"No, don't! Stop it!" Skeeter shouted. He gently stroked the horn. He was beginning to realize that the protrusion was bringing him great comfort. What once was an annoyance was now a pacifier.

"How is it yer gonna help save us humans? What kind of mission trip are you on, mister?" Skeeter asked.

"Look, it's no secret that Queen Daffodil is only trying to stir up hate. Her greed for money and power, the joy she feels from inflicting pain and suffering on others, is reprehensible. We, as a people, need to rise up above the hatred, and lead with peace, love, and science. Join us in turning the tides. We are working on solving this environmental crisis. We need people to stop fighting. We need people to cooperate with one another. There's a large group of scientists working on solutions to fix what mankind has damaged, but we need everyone on board if we're going to be able to change the destructive course we're currently on. We are desperately near the brink of no return."

Some of the militants nodded, others shrugged in agreement. A few grumbled in doubt and disbelief. Paraffin didn't want to lose their consent. He tried to keep the focus.

"Okay, look. Wouldn't it be better if everybody on the planet was concerned with the well-being of all the other souls on the planet? If each one of us made sure that others were doing okay, and we helped each other instead of competing with one another or fighting over who has more, there'd be more than enough to go around to each and every one of us."

"Who's really going to help me?" one of the militants asked. "I don't think that this guy here is really going to help me if I needed it," he said, pointing to one of the soldiers.

"Ahh, screw you," the soldier responded.

Junior Jr. interrupted, "Hey, fellas, hold on just a minute. Now, my daddy always said..."

He paused, struggling to remember what his daddy always said. "Let's see. My daddy always said something about the kindness of strangers. Well, I knowed the good book says some good words about kindness, too. Shoot, I can't remember 'zactly what he said."

Paraffin was losing his power to control the angry crowd. One of the militants, startled by the word 'Shoot,' mistakenly took it as a command to fire, accidentally pulling his rifle's trigger, shooting one of the other militants in the back. A young greenhorn private in the battalion twitched and fired off multiple rounds that hit other soldiers, militants, and himself – in both feet. Pretty soon, the goodwill Paraffin managed to create was destroyed. Bodies laid strewn about from the bloody firefight that ensued. Paraffin barely had the strength to engage his cloaking device to vanish into his surroundings.

Skeeter and Junior Jr. managed to escape unharmed. Skeeter hopped on Junior Jr.'s ATV, just as all four of his tires were shot out from the private's out-of-control trigger finger. By the time the firing stopped and the smoke cleared, barely a soul escaped injury. Both sides were primarily injured by friendly fire. Bullets meant for their enemies wounded or killed more of their own. The soldiers inflicted greater damage on the militants than the militants did on the soldiers. There were three times more soldiers than militants. Most of the soldiers were dead or seriously wounded, and almost all the militants were dead or would soon die from their injuries. Only Skeeter and Junior Jr. III escaped unharmed. They soon found themselves on a hilltop, hiding along with the opaque celestial being, Paraffin.

CHAPTER TWENTY-SIX

Both parties were a little surprised to see each other. Junior Jr. spoke first. "I think what you're saying makes sense, mister. And even though you zapped my cousin Skeeter in da foe-head and made him growd a hone, I think he'd agree with you, too."

"I do agree," Skeeter said, "and I'm growing strangely fond of this here horn. It…it feels…it feels like it's a part of me now." Skeeter paused to gently caress the new growth. "Now that I have a horn, I can't imagine what it was like not having one. Here, touch it if you want. It's starting to grow a light fuzz on it. It feels nice to touch."

"I don't want to touch your horn, Skeeter," Junior Jr.

said, turning to face Paraffin. "I want this spaceman here to tell us what we should do next. Most'f our kinfolk are lying in that field dead or dying, and I'm afraid if Queen Daffodil wants us dead, she'll kill us, too. 'Specially now that that field is full of her dead soldiers, too."

"I need to recharge," Paraffin said. "For the moment, we need to get as far away from here as we can. I think we should keep following the slope of this hill. If we continue moving uphill, we'll have a vantage point to see who, if anyone, is following us. Hopefully, we'll find a cave or some sort of area where we can hide and rest. I need about 12 hours, if possible, before my energy is fully restored – then I'll have my powers back. We should ditch your motor vehicle. It'll give us away if anyone comes looking for us. Plus, we'll be harder to track if we proceed on foot. Once my powers are restored, I'll be able to tele-transport us, or I can hide the three of us with my cloaking device."

The three comrades hid the ATV in a ravine and covered it with mud and brush. They proceeded up the long, slow slope of the hill, eventually cresting along the ridge where they were able to take refuge in a cave worn out from centuries of erosion. It was dank inside the cave, but a small fire dried out the dampness, staving off the cold throughout the night. All three of the men, each with some of their own provisions, along with food they foraged from the woods, were able to throw together a rather sumptuous smorgasbord for supper that evening. The half-moon rose early, visible in the dark blue sky just before darkness fell. Venus sat below the half-moon and a blanket of stars highlighted the distant heavens. Wispy clouds serenaded across the sky, eventually covering the moon and the stars. The three men laughed and swapped tales of their youth. The two cousins talked of their upbringing, and Paraffin answered questions about what it was like for him growing up on Earth. They began wondering why they wouldn't have been friends in the first place. For the most part, they had more in common than not – except that Paraffin was born in a petri dish and was sucked into this plane of existence from another universe, and Skeeter and Junior Jr. III were kinfolk twice over. Skeeter had a patch over one eye that wasn't actually damaged, and a horn, which he had now grown fond of. The felt was soft and soothing. It comforted Skeeter and made him less anxious. On the surface, Junior Jr. might not seem very bright, but was actually a thoughtful person and a bit of a deep thinker. He and Paraffin managed to find common ground on many topics.

Back at the palace, Queen Daffodil received word of the reported massacre. She sent out a search party that discovered the garrison had been gunned down, along with the dozen or so militants killed. Furious that something like this could happen, she sent forth a fury of troops to wreak torture and destruction on any innocent bystander or township they encountered.

After a day of rest and recharge, Paraffin sensed trouble was afoot. He decided it would be best to guide his new companions back in the direction of the gorge leading to The Crystal City. He sensed that he may need to run interference in case The Queen's blitzkrieg caught up with Ryder and the shaman.

Traveling in silence, Ryder and Nora arrived at the foot of a massive rainforest. Staring up at the centuries-old old-growth forest towering toward the sky, Nora thought of Jacob's ladder. Ryder was without words; it was impossible to express the overwhelming awe that was felt from the sight, the smell, and the sound of these magnificent trees. Ryder had lived an entire life in a filthy grey city, a place with no affect, no fresh food, or fresh water. Desolation was the norm. It was a place where most people couldn't afford food, water, or clean clothes. On this quest to deliver a sacred message, Ryder had experienced all kinds of natural wonders and beauties, but here, standing on the outskirts of this beautiful, lush rainforest, a tender place inside the heart sent shivers down the spine, and for the first time ever, the feeling of a power greater than mankind was realized.

"What's wrong? You stopped pedaling," Nora asked.

"I've never seen anything like this," Ryder said. "I've seen some amazing feats of nature recently, but this is like nothing I've ever imagined."

Ryder could smell the rich, luxuriant forest, the beautiful decay of the composting forest floor, and the wetness of the mammoth sequoias towering over them. Light shining through the canopy, like beams gleaming through stained glass windows of a cathedral, left geometric shapes that danced and swayed on the ground with each gentle breeze, similar to the reflection of a giant kaleidoscope. Ryder and

Nora felt as though they were entering a hallowed place. If they had been wearing hats, they would've been obliged to remove them. Ryder dismounted and slowly walked in. It was dizzying staring up at the tops of the giant trees. If not for the help of holding onto the handlebars, Ryder would've fallen over in stunned amazement.

"For many generations, my ancestors called this rainforest home," Nora said. "However, over recent generations, we have spread out far and wide, past the woods and plains where you and I met. My people have even dispersed as far as the deserts far to the southwest. I don't know the exact location of the place we're looking for, but as long as Queen Daffodil or any of her search parties don't detect us, I know I can guide us through this rainforest."

As Ryder and Nora entered the rainforest, Skeeter, Junior Jr. III, and Paraffin set off over the foothills and the scrub brush where they had been hiding. At that very moment, a new battalion – a more serious lot than the loafers who now lay dead, strewn about in a field – was quickly on its way to seek and impose The Queen's revenge. When Queen Daffodil heard about the skirmish in the woods between the militants and her soldiers, as well as some sort of strange creature, she sent out a massive force to retaliate.

Ryder, silent and reflective on the vision with Elizer, hadn't much to say until now. "So, what's it like living in a rainforest?"

"Well, I was raised in the woods not far from where we met. I used to visit my great-grandparents; they lived here in this very rainforest."

"Are they medicine people, too?"

"Not all of them. Each person in our tribe is a spiritual being, but not every one of them would be considered a shaman."

"What's it like growing up with a shaman for a father? Was your mother also a shaman?"

"It was normal for me. No, my mom wasn't a shaman, just my father. But his sister was a shaman, too. Our tribe lived under their guidance and leadership. They were respected leaders in our community. I've always looked up to my father and I've always admired him. He's a great person, but I've never aspired to be a shaman or medicine person. He always said that I had the gift. Ever since I was a child, I've had visions and a strong intuition that often proved to be true. I feel anointed now with my father's blessings, and for him to send me on this pilgrimage with you is a privilege. It's like the passing of the totem."

They walked in silence until Ryder finally asked a question that wouldn't go away.

"Nora, that kiss back in the kiva after the trance…what was that about?"

"Well, I'm not sure. I felt strangely drawn to you and you looked like you needed a kiss," she said.

"It was strange, but it felt natural," Ryder told her.

"It felt electric. As I kissed you, I had a flash from a past life."

They both looked at each other and Nora continued.

"I had a strong feeling of déjà vu when we kissed. I'm actually having one right now. Do you believe in past lives,

Ryder?"

"I don't know. I've been so worried about trying to survive and stay alive in this life that I haven't given it much thought. I guess it's possible. I mean, now that I think about it, I don't see why not."

Nora smiled and said, "I think it *is* possible and I feel like we've known each other in a past life."

"Okay, maybe we have. I can't say for certain…I'd be lying if I said I did."

Ryder paused for a moment before continuing. "I must admit, the first time I laid eyes on you standing back in the woods before you took me to meet your father, that was a strangely familiar moment. It was as if I already knew you or my mind's eye recognized you when I first saw you.

Walking in the radiant sunlight of the rainforest, smiling, gently holding each other's fingertips, time and concerns drifted away.

"Back at the kiva, when I came out of my hallucinatory trance, the first thing I saw was you. And then you leaned over and kissed me as if we'd done that a thousand times before."

"See! I felt it, too. That's what I mean. That's what I'm talking about!"

Ryder nodded in agreement. Nora closed her eyes and leaned in for another kiss, but before she could reach Ryder's lips, the sounds of voices from a portable communication device interrupted them. Ryder stood up to pedal and Nora hopped on the seat, grabbing hold of Ryder's hips as they made a quick getaway without being noticed. Once they felt like they were at a relatively safe distance away, they stopped to regroup.

"We've got to do something, Ryder. If there's a search party already upon us, we're in grave danger."

"What should we do?"

"There's no way we can take on an entire regiment by ourselves, at least not head-on...but we might disarm and disorient them in some way."

"How can we do that?"

"My father has taught me many incantations handed down orally through centuries of our generations. I've been given the words to sacred prayers as well as formulas to special potions. I've been part of many ceremonies that have prepared me for this very moment. I now realize my true purpose on this planet. Just as our kiss gave me familiar feelings from a hundred lives ago, so it is that this moment is before us. Now, I need you to quickly gather as many alder berries as you can find."

Nora began rifling through a beaded leather pouch she wore around her neck. From it, she produced a smaller pouch of sulfur powder, a feather, a bag of mixed herbs, including shaved almond and nutmeg, a string of wooden beads, some smooth river rocks, and several small colorful gemstones. Ryder soon returned with a shirt full of alder berries. Nora found a large stone protruding from the ground. A smooth curved oval indention made it perfect for what she needed. Placing the alder berries in the natural trough, she ground the berries into a paste using a stone she found that fit comfortably in the palm of her hand. Mixing the sulfur into the paste, she then added the herbs and shaved almonds and nutmeg. She chewed on the bits of almond before spitting them onto her fingers then rubbing it into the mixture. Gathering little twigs and small pieces of bark, she built a small mound next to the ingredients resting inside the mortar. She laid out the gemstones in a semi-circle near the trough. Holding the river rocks and beads, Nora raised her hands up to her forehead and back to her heart as she began reciting the incantation. After several minutes of repeating the chant, she pulled a knife from a leather sheath that she also wore around her neck, and she struck a piece of flint, igniting the contents on the rock. Holding out her hands and looking up to the sky, Nora continued with the prayer, repeating the phrase in an ancient tongue over and over again. The chant was a magic spell used with the intention to repel enemy combatants. Its purpose was to keep the pair within a protective force field. It also had powers to confuse the troops and render their electronics useless.

The spell was to leave the troops and their leaders confused, almost amnesiac. Many of the soldiers became sick to their stomachs, suffering with extreme headaches and nausea, as if suddenly struck with an epidemic. The spell worked and the entire battalion felt ill and confused. Radio transmission back to their base was futile, as none of the electronics were working properly. Other machinery, trucks, and weaponry began breaking down as well. Without even knowing they had been attacked, the brigade retreated back to the base, leaving Ryder and Nora free to roam the rainforest in search of their unknown destination.

After walking for a while, neither saying a word, Nora noticed something. A sound.

"Do you hear that?" she whispered.

"Hear what?"

"Shhh, it sounds like water."

"I only hear the wind."

"Come on. Follow me," Nora directed, as she let go of Ryder's hand and took off toward the sound.

Ryder paused then spoke. "Oh yeah, there it is. Now I hear it…and I can smell it, too."

Nora led Ryder through some brush and a thicket that was difficult to maneuver with the bike. After a minor struggle, they managed to get through, coming out of the thicket and into a shallow meadow that led to a clear river with a waterfall falling like a pure, reflective sheet of water. They stood in wonder, staring at it, gasping in awe at its beauty.

"Oh my gosh! This is beautiful," Ryder exclaimed.

Nora lit some sage, closed her eyes, and began to slip into a brief trance. Meditating for a moment with her eyes closed, she eventually said, "I think we've stumbled onto the entrance of whatever it is that you're looking for."

"What should we do?" Ryder asked.

"I think we should hang out and go for a swim. We might even camp here for the night. I have a feeling that if we wait, they'll find us instead of us having to find them."

Nora looked up at the cliff from where the water fell.

"I'm not sure if we have what we need to scale that wall

across the river, but I have a feeling that this is where the hidden city lies. I think there's a better way to get there than straight up that cliff," she said, undressing and preparing to jump in the water naked. "Let's soak up some of this beauty and relax here for the rest of the day. I bet the answer will reveal itself before long."

CHAPTER TWENTY-SEVEN

This time, the military personnel Queen Daffodil deployed were of the utmost ruthless nature. They spared no pity on any living creature they encountered. Furnishings, belongings of any kind, crops, trees, plants, men, women, children, pets, and animals – nothing was spared from being torched, tortured, or decimated. They destroyed everything and left in their wake the stench of rotting flesh and gasoline. Queen Daffodil, with her psychic abilities, began homing in on Paraffin and his companions. However, Ryder and Nora's carefree, relaxed nature did not register on The Queen's psychic radar. She perceived nothing from their peaceful vibrations.

Through her abilities, Queen Daffodil directed the special forces in the direction she perceived the threat to be. The troops were only a few hours away from overrunning Paraffin, Skeeter, and Junior Jr.'s position. In all likelihood, after eliminating these three, The Queen's brigade would probably continue their blitzkrieg, moving into the rainforest and causing irreparable damage to the ancient sequoias. It would be catastrophic if they were to discover Ryder and Nora, and then stop them from achieving their mission, which could lead to the discovery of The Crystal City, destroying all the hard work of The People's People to restore the planet's environment.

Paraffin knew that he and his new companions were being followed. He knew there was no way he and the two cousins could overtake the soldiers peacefully. He also knew that if he wasn't able to avert their advances, Ryder and the mission were in jeopardy, and would most likely end in failure or death. He also couldn't help but wonder if Ryder and the shaman were being followed and needed help. The heightened danger made it more difficult for him to meditate and follow his gut. To find Ryder and the shaman, Paraffin was concerned of the risk in leading the army toward the direction he believed they would be traveling. He wondered if he should be a distraction, a decoy, and try leading the troops away from Ryder and Nora. Once he cleared his mind, his intuition guided him to do just that. He chose to trust that Ryder and Nora would be safe on their own and that it would be more helpful to lead the troops away from the rainforest.

Paraffin needed to be sure The Queen's men would follow him, but not too closely. Starting a fire with a pile of dried leaves and scraps of wood, he knew the smoke would be a good way to alert the soldiers that someone wasn't far away. Paraffin, Skeeter, and Junior Jr. didn't stick around. They took off in the opposite direction of the oncoming army, only to circle back around behind the army. Paraffin knew the soldiers would be confused since following the tracks would lead them back to their own regiment. Paraffin and the boys could've lost the troops completely, but Paraffin knew that he needed to keep guiding them in the opposite direction from where Ryder was traveling. After a long day of marching in circles following their own tracks, the soldiers camped for the night. The next morning, Paraffin made it easy for them to find his new course, purposely leading them in the direction of his choosing.

For several days, Paraffin kept up the chase, leaving not-so-subtle clues behind for the soldiers to follow. The celestial being was able to mislead the army into thinking they were stalking six or seven people instead of only three. He scribbled and drew on ledger sheets he produced from the sleeves of his magic robe, dropping more clues to confuse and trick the soldiers into believing they were discovering cryptic bits of important information, none of it true. Paraffin also wanted the trackers to believe the illusion that they were on the trail of something or somebody who was of the upmost importance. He didn't want them to lose interest or give up the search. Yet, he couldn't allow himself to be captured too soon, for they may realize that the real threat was somewhere else.

"How long do you reckon we can keep this up?" Skeeter asked.

"I'm hoping we can lead them into a ravine. I know of one that's still a day or two away. If we can get them trapped and confused deep inside this ravine, I believe we can finally lose them and be on our way back in the direction of the rainforest without them being able to find us. First, though, I need a day or two to recuperate and meditate so I can recharge and see if I can pick up on any psychic messages. I'm hoping my intentions will give me a clear message once I've cleared my inner chatter."

"Where do you expect to sit for two days with an army of soldiers chasing us? They're bound to be getting pretty angry with us. I don't expect a pleasant outcome if they were to find us."

"Don't you worry. I have a plan. There's a nice spot up on the hill overlooking this ravine. If we can get there before they catch up to us, we can hide in a cave I know that's formed in the limestone. I have enough power for us to use my cloaking device once we're in the cave. That will protect us from being noticed in case any of the soldiers come near us. I can make it appear as though the entrance is made of solid rock. Even if someone were to lean up against the opening, it would feel like a solid object. I doubt they'll stay in the area very long. It's rough terrain and it wouldn't be a comfortable place for them to stop and camp or rest."

"What would happen if they *did* stay in the area for an extended period of time?" Junior Jr. asked.

"I have a few other tricks up my robe. If they were to happen upon us for an extended stay, I would attempt to keep us invisible long enough to slip away. The trouble is my powers are liable to be dimming if I keep up a shield of deception for an extended period of time."

Paraffin could see the doubtful looks on their faces, and offered Skeeter and Junior Jr. some reassurance. "I feel good about this. Don't worry. They aren't going to stay long. Come on now, let's get going. We need to hurry and get away from here. I have a feeling they're kicking it into double-time. We should double-time it, too."

CHAPTER TWENTY-EIGHT

Nora and Ryder followed a narrow path through the meadow leading them to the river. Rocks jutting out to a sandbar made it easy for them to ford across a narrow bend in the stream. After making a lean-to out of fallen limbs and scrub oak, they undressed and took a swim. There were still a couple of hours before dusk when some visitors arrived. They walked into the camp unnoticed, barely making a sound. Two young men and a woman twice their age were all dressed in earth tones, making it easy for them to blend into the environment. They crept up on Ryder and Nora without any notice. Even Nora, with her psychic intuition, was surprised.

After a brief stare-off, the strangers said, "We've been expecting you."

The two younger men began dismantling the lean-to, dispersing the pieces in a random manner, leaving no trace of what it once was.

"We don't want to leave any evidence of someone being here in case The Queen's forces search the area," the woman, whose name was Raiyn, told them. "You there…," she said, nodding at Ryder. "You'll need to carry that bike so we don't leave any tire tracks behind. Don't worry, you won't need to carry it very far. We have a secret entrance over here."

The young men followed far enough behind that the others couldn't see them. They wanted to make sure no one was following them and to smooth over any footprints they might have left behind. Raiyn led Ryder and Nora to a second waterfall that fell into the creek feeding the river flowing into the larger waterfall. It wasn't obvious, but there was a narrow passage behind the smaller waterfall that led to a gigantic boulder that would move to one side when a secret lever was pushed into place. There was just enough room to squeeze through the opening, which led to a dank tunnel lit by solar-powered lights that were triggered on by their motions. In case of an emergency, you could turn them off and on by clapping twice.

"I have a message I need to give your council leaders," Ryder told them. "I don't fully understand it, but it's very important."

"My council leaders are expecting you. Right this way,"

Raiyn directed, leading the pair over to a ladder that led up to a manhole cover.

Raiyn paused, looked at Ryder, and said, "You're going to need to leave your bicycle down here."

"I'd rather not."

"It's just for the time being, I promise. We can get a rope and hoist it up, but it might not fit through the opening. Plus, it's imperative you get in touch with Crystal and Grace right away. I'll have my sons take your bike the long way around – up the ramp and out of the tunnel."

"Okay, I suppose I can trust you," Ryder said half-jokingly before proceeding to climb up the ladder.

CHAPTER TWENTY-NINE

Skeeter, Junior Jr. III, and Paraffin reached the ravine far in advance of the troops that were tracking them, but by the time the troops arrived, they had called for reinforcements. There were two more brigades moving in, as well as surveillance drones, armored vehicles, and fighter jets circling about the area, making a wide swath in hopes of finding them. Paraffin had led the search team on such a drawn-out chase that tempers flared and patience had run thin amongst Her Majesty's army. The soldiers were determined to annihilate, in the worst possible way, the culprits who forced them into this exhaustive pursuit.

Paraffin, Skeeter, and Junior Jr. III rounded up some

provisions from an abandoned cabin they discovered on their way to the cave overlooking the ravine. They prepared to hunker down in the cave for as long as possible to avoid capture. To pass the time, they played games like Charades and 20 Questions. Meanwhile, outside the cave, hidden by Paraffin's cloaking ability, the sound of army helicopters, tanks, and commanders barking out orders could be heard circling all around them.

"I wish you could hypnotize them and change their perspective like you did us and that other group of soldiers," Junior Jr. said.

Paraffin took a breath and said, "That works in smaller numbers, but I'm not sure I can do that with a battalion as large as the one that's currently following us. Plus, now there's jets, tanks, and a large number of foot soldiers. The numbers may be too great for me to control at once. This is going to require some deep meditation. I need to recharge and summon all my abilities to enable me to come up with a solution. I don't think my cloaking abilities are going to be able to sustain us for too much longer."

"Somehow, we need to convince these army boys that their methods are all wrong. Help them to see the light of goodwill and commonality in all of mankind," Junior Jr. said.

"Yeah, like you did for us," Skeeter added. He rubbed the felt on his horn as he spoke. Touching the soft felt of his horn brought him comfort, especially whenever he was nervous or anxious. It was like a security blanket. He continued to grow strangely fond of his horn. The animosity he initially felt when he grew the horn no longer existed; it now made him feel safe and secure. He even stopped wearing his fake eyepatch. He completely discarded it, throwing it away into the dark side of the cave. The lightheartedness the group enjoyed when they first took refuge in the cave was beginning to subside. No longer did they tell jokes and play games. The fun ceased once they realized the soldiers were not simply passing through.

"They must have a good reason for coming to this area," Paraffin said. "It could be heat-seeking radar locating us or some other device. But I think it might be for some other reason. Perhaps Queen Daffodil's crystal ball has been tracking us. Once we disappeared from her vision through her magic sphere, she must have alerted the troops, figuring out that this area is where we're most likely hiding. She probably realizes that we have cloaking abilities, too. I don't know for certain if she's even aware of me or if she even knows I exist. Either way, I think she's figured out that she's dealing with a special entity."

"How long do you think we have?" Skeeter asked.

"I know my cloaking device should hold up for about another two or three days…unless they start blasting the area directly with any sort of laser beams or heavy frequencies, in which case it would create a ripple effect in my shield, causing it to fall apart like putty."

"That doesn't sound good," Junior Jr. replied.

"Well, the odds of that happening are pretty slim. If they were to blast a wide swath of frequency lasers, it would affect them and their electronic gear. The only way it would work is if, for some reason, they directed a beam straight at the opening of the cave. Our barrier wouldn't last long if that were the case. I'm going to need to meditate and go into a trance for up to 48 hours. And I need you guys to keep staying positive and focused. The more positive energy we transmit, the less likely we are to draw their psychic attention toward us. I'm going to get you to cut, shave, and tie together this wood that's in here. We need to make shields large enough to cover our entire bodies in case we need to run for it. Just keep telling yourselves that you're going to be okay. The more you believe it, the more likely it will come true. There's an ancient Vedic text that's several thousands of years old that teaches us that the most powerful tool we have for healing is our mind, body, and spirit. We are our own healers. As is the atom, so is the universe. As is the microcosm, so is the macrocosm. As is the human body, so is the cosmic body. Ultimate healing is complete harmony between your body and the body of the physical universe."

Junior Jr., nodding affirmatively, replied, "Wow, that's heavy."

"Those aren't my words; they're from an ancient Vedic text that's thousands of years old," Paraffin said.

Paraffin got comfortable in a cool, dark spot next to a wall in the cave. Sitting cross-legged on the floor, he lit some herbs (frankincense and sage) and started rubbing a wooden handle around a Nepalese bowl, which produced a hypnotic tone. He began to enter into a trance. After chanting and playing the bowl for several hours, he eventually laid down with his arms across his forehead. He moaned, rocking back and forth, and side to side, before drifting off into an astral projection. He remained there for a day and a half, only coming to slightly whenever Skeeter would lift his head in an effort to have him drink a few drops of water squeezed from a handkerchief.

In his dream, Paraffin saw an opening in this plane of existence, parting like a brightly-lit vagina. He was able to walk back through the light into his previously existing realm. As if looking through the doors of perception or the windows of time, he witnessed grave dangers and persecution to many inhabitants of his host planet, Earth. He witnessed death and destruction, birth and life, over and over again. He witnessed the gruesome and grizzly death of a young being, which he interpreted to be himself. He grew ashen with fear and became so anxious that his throat started drying out. Breathing became a struggle. The grip in his throat, now as dry as the desert sands, tightened like a noose from the gallows of the Grim Reaper.

Finally giving in and accepting his own death, the grip loosened. He was able to breathe easily again. No longer fearing death, Paraffin traveled freely inside this astral projection. He saw a light at the end of a long, narrow tunnel that twisted and turned, similar to a cosmic fallopian tube. He saw what he believed to be Ryder and Nora reaching their destination. Even though he had never met them, he saw the faces of Crystal, Grace, the scientists, Norman and Orville Poff, along with a team of scientists, sitting at an expansive desk with computer screens, much like that of a space center's launch site. He witnessed moments of stress and fear throughout the room on the faces of those working.

He saw elation and cheers as hands went up in the air and hugs were given to everyone around the room.

But then, a sinister concern came over him – he realized he was responsible for the lives of Skeeter and Junior Jr. He thought up a plan of deception. His only chance was to give himself away in the hope that in the chaos that would ensue, the boys could escape.

However, another notion just crossed his mind. If he were able to control the minds and freeze the action of some of the soldiers, others may hesitate on reacting and attacking, perhaps even changing their minds and perspectives, too.

When Paraffin came out of the trance, he felt rested and clearheaded. It didn't take long for fear to creep back into his psyche. Paraffin reminded himself to stay focused and to follow his gut. He reminded himself to stay tuned in to what he wanted to happen, not what he didn't want to happen.

CHAPTER THIRTY

Crystal and Grace were eagerly waiting to meet the two travelers. They had been tracking them and were anticipating their arrival for some time. The excitement was felt by everyone throughout the chamber. No one knew what to expect, but they had a sense that the information Ryder and Nora had would be crucial in transforming the advancement of their efforts to save Earth.

Climbing through the portal and into the annex of The Crystal City, Ryder looked up and saw Crystal standing next to Grace and the team of scientists. As if in a bizarre dream, Ryder and Crystal locked eyes and experienced the same strange sensation of déjà vu. There had been so many instances of déjà vu lately that both of them equated it to yet another prodigious occurrence. Ryder thought it was just another past life remembrance. What they didn't know, and what they would never know or ever come to realize, is that they were connected in this lifetime by having the same father. Even though they had never met, they were siblings fathered by the same man, a renegade miner who fathered many children with numerous different women. Some were wives, some were girlfriends, many of them were simply one-night stands. Ryder's mom met the miner, the biological father, before meeting the man she married, who Ryder always called 'Dad'. Ryder never knew anything about the man.

Crystal didn't know much about her father either. All she knew was that he was a miner, nothing more. Her mom said they had been together for only a short time and then he disappeared. Before she knew it, she was pregnant. The man was a playboy, young and immature. Not cruel, but unreliable. He had dark, brooding eyes that women couldn't resist…and many boys, for that matter. Apparently, he preferred the company of men, but was always afraid to admit it, for fear that he would be beaten or thrown down a shaft of one of the mines where he worked. Neither Crystal nor Ryder's mom knew the many secrets of this man, who went by the name of Jake. He later drifted off into oblivion, a cosmic grifter of sorts, possibly dying due to his careless lifestyle. Ryder's mom didn't know the man or who he really was. She never spoke of him or uttered his name. And neither did Crystal's mom.

After a brief introduction, everyone sat down for a healthy lunch of fish and vegetables. They explained to each other what they knew up to this point about the environment and the possible solutions. Ryder and Nora were famished, and it was a relief to replenish themselves with a hearty meal. After lunch, Ryder told them everything Noah Billingsworth had explained about the concept of individuals having their own cosmic element. Just as everyone's DNA was a unique fingerprint, everyone's cosmic element was their ethereal DNA, unique only to themselves. And just like any combination of chemical elements on the periodic table, individuals, when combined with certain other individuals, could produce a specific chemical reaction, thus inventing a completely new chemical element, forming a very special and unique reaction.

Ryder paused, looked directly at Crystal, and continued. "Apparently, you and I have a cosmic element equation that's unique and completely necessary to combine in order to send a psychic message to the space colonies on Mars. Earth has been shut off from communication with the space colonies for so long, we don't even know if humans on Mars still exist. Or if they do still exist, they may think that humans here no longer exist, that we were wiped out from the great volcanic explosions from Yellowstone, along with all the years of war and famine. They may think that all of us, the inhabitants here on Earth, have perished. For all we know, they have also perished…but most likely, they're still alive, unless there's been an unforeseen disaster on Mars as well."

"Well, what is it that we need to do?" Crystal asked.

"What's the message we need to send?"

"The science you and your team have developed to speed up Earth's recovery has already been tremendously helpful. Supposedly, there's a substance only on Mars that will enable us to speed up the recovery of Earth's atmosphere and environment to quantum proportions."

"What is it?"

"It's a type of carbon nitrate similar to, but unlike anything we've seen here on Earth. I can't read it, and I certainly don't understand it, but Noah Billingsworth has given me the written formula on how to incorporate this substance into a mechanism to make this possible. Once we have it, we can make it a reality. Noah Billingsworth has designed a device that will amplify and reverse the incremental damage that has been constantly happening to the air and water on our planet for centuries. It will be a conduit to the recovery, but on an exponential level."

"Okay, but then what? After the mass eruptions from the bombs and volcanoes here on Earth, we haven't had the capability to launch a rocket to send for help or to transport refugees to Mars. They've also lost the ability to communicate with us or send a spacecraft back to Earth."

"Noah Billingsworth has sent with me an equation on how to dematerialize matter – solid objects. We have plans to also develop this for humans. This equation is a formula that will enable us to dematerialize objects and send them wherever we want. We'll be able to do this faster than the speed of light. First things first, once they receive our initial message, we can send them this information for the minerals we need and how to go about dematerializing them and sending them here to these specific coordinates on Earth."

"It's going to blow their minds! How do you expect them to receive this initial message?"

"Before the explosion at Yellowstone, which was the nail in the coffin of an already-exasperated environmental situation with our planet, there was one nation that had developed the most advanced inner space monitoring detection equipment ever built – and that was the Cuban colony on Mars. Noah thinks our best chance will be to send a message there. It won't just be the combination of Crystal and me sending this cosmic telepathic message; we need Grace, Nora, and seven others from your community. Some of the scientists here and other individuals with a profound spiritual nature from your community."

"How will we know it's working?"

"Noah Billingsworth told me that we'll definitely know. There will be a noticeable electrical charge in the atmosphere. He said we'll feel it. It'll be undeniable. Our messages will infiltrate their network, and our thoughts will be turned into words on their radar screens."

"How long will this take?"

"That I can't tell you."

"Why not?"

"Because I don't know. Noah Billingsworth didn't tell me how long this process would take. I didn't think to ask him."

Outside, a ferocious wind began to blow. The walls and floors of the room creaked and popped alive, like a living spirit.

Crystal, Grace, Ryder, Nora, and Orville and Norman Poff, along with a combination of the most respected spiritual leaders and scientists in their community, came together for a telepathic interstellar celestial message aimed specifically at the Cuban colony on Mars. The 11 members of the equation sat in a circle outside in a clearing under the stars within the forest. The stars were extra brilliant that night due to the dark skies of the new moon. Time passed slowly until time itself became still, and everything in its existence seemed motionless. Time was irrelevant, and the 11 human components of this cosmic equation focused on one thought, one mantra with clear intention, sending this message through space like a radio signal of thought and purpose.

After several hours of hypnotic, motionless thought and focus, there was a receiver, an individual of the Cuban colony on the planet Mars. Suddenly, a radar screen began getting a signal. It started beeping a sound like Morse Code, creating a pattern when amplified. When it was transcribed, the message read:

[illegible], I am on a linear track.
You are a wavelength.
Our paths will cross at certain junctures.

The message had to be interpreted from English to Spanish because as it turned out, it was the Cuban space colony on Mars that received and transcribed the cosmic message. After the first cryptic message, the cast of 11 meditators sent specific information about the minerals and substances they needed from Mars to be sent to Earth. Ryder unknowingly possessed and understood the specific instructions from a mental implant, similar to hypnosis, which Noah Billingsworth had installed in Ryder's brain. He also installed instructions on how to dematerialize the substances and how to send them through the cosmos to this specific location. There was a time in history when America worried about Cuba launching rockets that would destroy American cities and possibly the world, but now, Cuba was going to send a cosmic rocket that would protect America. In it would be a shipment of molecules that would materialize into a substance that could save the entire planet. The hours passed like mirrored moments, tiny flakes of time that seemed to be an eternity, reflecting endlessly off each other. Other scientists and members of the local council waited outside the meditation circle. Waiting in anticipation, hopeful for some kind of sign that the message was not only received, but understood.

Suddenly and without warning, an electrical charge was felt by each of the meditators. The electrical charge passed through Ryder first then through Crystal, emanating one by one in rapid succession through each person in the circle of eleven. From the sky erupted a massive electrical charge. Lightning crackled and thunder clapped. Bolts of lightning branched out into a wide, colorful display – a cosmic aurora borealis that spanned the entire 33.9 million miles. from Earth to Mars. The message was received, transcribed, and understood.

And so, the process had begun. Soon, the first successful attempt at transporting matter into a cosmic molecular form, traveling 20 times faster than the speed of light, and then re-transformed into its previous solid nature, was complete and successful.

But before it was complete and the healing of the planet intensified, there were still mass atrocities being committed. The lives and safety of Paraffin, Skeeter, and Junior Jr. III were still in a peerless and perilous situation.

CHAPTER THIRTY-ONE

The Queen's army was swiftly moving in. The ground trembled, as if in fear, from the roar and rumbling of the tanks outside the cave. Pebbles and pieces of rock from the cave's walls and ceiling crumbled to the ground, rolling across the floor like tears falling down a cheek.

"Alright, buddy. What's the plan?" Junior Jr. asked.

"Yeah, I gotta admit…I'm getting a little scared," Skeeter said. "My horn is beginning to throb like it's trying to tell me something. I'm getting a powerfully pounding headache."

Paraffin could feel the cloaking shield weakening. When he closed his eyes, he saw static electricity wavering out of focus like an old television. Paraffin, basking in the afterglow from his visions during his astral projection, feared no outcome.

He explained, "Well, gentlemen, just sit tight. We have enough energy in our shields to last until dark. Once the sun sets, we'll sneak out under the cover of darkness. We should be able to blend in and make our escape after nightfall. In the meantime, I'm going to continue to rest. You fellas should eat up the rest of the provisions that are left. Once we flee, it may be a while before you get anything hearty to eat. Let's share some of this special honey I have. It'll give us clean, pure energy that will help keep us healthy and alert. We're going to have to travel fast and light once we sneak out of here."

Paraffin, with his back straight, sitting cross-legged on the floor, closed his eyes, conserving every ounce of energy as the sun moved across the sky, setting in the direction of the advancing army. Skeeter, Junior Jr., and Paraffin were planning to blend in with the troops that were steadily advancing to the west.

Once darkness fell, Paraffin was able to release the cloaking imagery, and the three men carefully and nonchalantly walked out of the cave. Skeeter was careful to keep his head down, drawing as little attention as possible to his horn. His cohorts fastened some gauze around Skeeter's head to appear less horn-like and more headgear-like. It was not easy for the trio to find an opening to sneak away from the troops. The battalion spread wide in all directions. Eventually, in a wooded area, dark with shadows, the three were able to separate themselves from the militants and the soldiers of The Queen's brigade.

"What are we going to do?" Skeeter asked. "There's no way we can combat such a large group of soldiers."

"No, we can't fight a group this large," Junior Jr. added.

"I have a plan," Paraffin reassured them. "When I was in my meditative trance, a vision came to me with a solution. If I am to implement this, I'm going to need you fellas to continue on without me. I need you boys to carry a message through to Ryder and the others, so they'll understand what I have done. Our physical time in these physical bodies is limited. Mine may be nearing its finale. Our souls will carry on. It's become clear to me, as I understand it, that my time to leave this body is approaching. I believe I have one more magnificent feat of thaumaturgy to pull off before I go."

With puzzled expressions on their faces, Skeeter and Junior Jr. looked at each other to see if the other understood.

"Where are you going to go?" Junior Jr. asked.

"Yeah, you can't leave us." Skeeter said.

"I'll still be with you always, but my physical existence will change. It will be up to you to carry the news to the others. We're going to continue to lead the army away from the rainforest and The Crystal City. We will lead them into the desert horizons far into the southwest. Once we outflank them, we'll circle around and surprise them by taking them head-on, face to face."

"What? Why?" Skeeter and Junior Jr. asked in unison.

"We can't attack such a large army in a frontal assault," Junior Jr. said. "We should just slowly pick them off one by one from a distance, guerrilla warfare-style. We can figure out a way to poison their water or their supplies."

"Yeah, we gotta be stealth-like," Skeeter added, as he slowly stroked at the felt on his horn, helping to calm his nervousness.

"No, trust me. We won't survive those types of tactics. I have a plan, one last feat of cosmic trickery that will hopefully change the minds of these misguided souls."

For almost a week, day and night, Paraffin and the two cousins manipulated themselves, circumventing The Queen's army. Their deception was working. They tricked the soldiers into believing that they were in pursuit of a much greater foe. The army was certain that an advantageous outcome was imminent.

Finally, the day arrived.

Paraffin knew that this was it. It was a brisk morning. A biting chill was in the air and dewdrops dotted the earth. Circles of prisms, each containing the reflection of the morning sky, sparkled from the ground. The universe was encapsulated in tiny droplets of water. One hundred and fifty million kilometers away, the sun was in command, warming the desert terrain that lay ahead. Sparse, wispy clouds lined the dark blue skies. Unsuspecting troops slowly stirring were not overly alarmed and didn't feel the least bit threatened at the surprise that was about to occur.

Paraffin whispered to his companions, "What you are about to witness is not the end, but the beginning. I will still be with you in here," he said, pointing to his heart. He tilted his head back, then with palms open to the sky, he said, "I'm about to transform myself into pure sentience. In doing so, I intend to change the destructive nature within the souls of each of these soldiers following us. I intend to open their hearts to help them see that we are all one and the same. I hope to get them to stop the fighting and killing, and to focus their energy on helping one another. Within us, we are all love, but training, manipulation, and a negative mindset, much of it fueled by greed and hate, has turned so many of us against each other. It serves no one any good. We can live in peace and harmony by simply *being* peace and harmony with ourselves and those around us…but to do this one last marvel, I'll be expending this body and then taking on a new form. When I do, I'll need the two of you to take over where I'm leaving off."

Junior Jr. and Skeeter were keenly focused. Skeeter stopped rubbing his horn and stood straight at attention.

"If I can change the negative will of these soldiers, I'll need the two of you to lead them in the service of good. Ryder, the shaman, and the scientist I saw in my vision are going to need physical help in rebuilding the infrastructure of the planet. There will always be the likes of Queen Daffodil and those who continue to follow her. But she *must* be brought to justice, and her followers must be persuaded to change their destructive ways. They must learn to change their hate into love. Hate does not conquer hate, love conquers hate. Darkness and light, the stars and moons will still exist."

As Paraffin, Junior Jr., and Skeeter crested the hill and walked towards the army's camp, most of the foot soldiers were still rubbing sleep out of their eyes or tending to their breakfast rations divvied out in mess kits previously owned by dead soldiers. As the odd trio approached the camp, they were surprised by what they saw. In spite of the recent developments in war and technology, the signs of decimation to the Queen's forces were more than apparent. Many of the soldiers were old men or boys who were too young to be away from their mothers. The old men wore the masks of death. The young boys wore faces etched in fear and despair. There were still armored vehicles, tanks and planes doing sorties, but much of the artillery and supplies were toted on wooden carts pulled by slaves or malnourished animals barely clinging to life. Oxen and horses so starved that their skin draped over their bones like bedsheets hung over barren tree branches to dry.

The trio sauntered right down the middle of a well-worn dirt road, like they were on a stroll down the promenade, window shopping and taking in the sights and sounds of vendors that existed in civilizations long ago. They walked in stride as if there were not a care or danger in the world. Murmurs and disturbed mumblings mixed with guffaws and laughter could be heard around the camp, as the odd-looking trio marched toward them. Demands to halt were shouted.

An armed sentry, followed by several more armed guards, stepped into the road exclaimed, "Who now? Hold up! State your business."

Paraffin's nature was so calm that neither Junior Jr. or Skeeter felt any sense of alarm or worry. Skeeter didn't even need to stroke his horn for comfort.

Pointing their weapons, the soldiers shouted, "Stop right there!"

Raising their arms, the soldiers began to take aim as the three misfits continued to approach.

"I say, stop right there! I'm not going to tell you again."

Paraffin raised his palm from within his robe as he spoke to the man. "Greetings, hello. Nice to see you."

This welcoming puzzled the soldiers, yet they did not let down their guard.

"Isn't it a lovely day?" Paraffin asked.

"State your business!"

"Well, we're here to encourage you warriors to focus your energy on healing rather than destruction. There have been times in our lives when it was helpful and necessary for armies to mount and protect against tyranny. Sometimes armies help feed and distribute food in war-torn nations or after grave tragedies or natural disasters. But when armies are used to attack innocent civilians, usually under the orders of a corrupt government or dictator who only has their best interest at heart, attacking innocent people and nations who they call villains – villains that are merely created to justify their own means…" Paraffin paused, searching for the right words to say. "We're only here to try and convince you to lay down your arms in a call for peace. People, time and time again, have tried to solve problems with force. But peace, love, understanding, compassion, and kindness are simple and much better solutions."

"Kill them!" a voice shouted from the crowd of infantrymen watching the situation unfold.

"It's a trick! After them!" another voice yelled. No order was given, but multiple shots rang out, leading to a rapid succession of machine-gun fire.

Paraffin went into survival mode and instantly put up a shield that repelled every bullet. The earth shook violently as mortar fire exploded around them. The concussions from tank cannons firing multiple rounds directly at them nearly knocked Paraffin off his feet. He barely got an extra layer of his protective energy shield over them in time, saving them from the sudden onslaught. However, he felt his shield bruise.

He could hardly fend off the attack when he suddenly noticed Skeeter lying unconscious, motionless on the ground. He was very pale. Paler than normal. He was curled up in a fetal position, lifeless, yet looked peaceful. Paraffin's multiple hearts sank. He almost let go of his powers, which would have ensured the death of all three of them. He felt responsible for keeping these two creatures alive, and now it appeared that he failed to do so. Skeeter, who was once a bigoted, hateful, ignorant bumpkin, had changed his ways and outlook on life. He found his tender heart and was ready to share that experience with every other sentient being on the planet. Skeeter had experienced many things since he and Junior Jr. met Paraffin. Paraffin taught Skeeter a new way of seeing mankind and the world. After witnessing the senseless killings of others, it prompted them both to change. They had learned to think of others as themselves. They were now aware of how everyone's life and well-being were interconnected, and that the smallest actions of kindness or hate can have a profound impact on the world.

"Like ripples of water, the simplest of actions can affect others," Paraffin once told them. "We are all components of the same organism."

Skeeter and Junior Jr. were ready to make a difference and had changed for the betterment of others. Now, Skeeter lay there, lifeless. His pale face was illuminated by the glow from his horn, which had grown flushed with blood, like a beacon of an innocent life.

Paraffin let go of his feelings and turned his attention back to the troubles at hand.

"Please, gentlemen," he said softly. It was difficult to summon the energy to speak, as every bit of Paraffin's core was in use to protect from the shelling.

He repeated, "Please, gentlemen. We mean you no harm."

That statement stoked the ire and mistrust of the soldiers. They began to bombard an even heavier barrage of weaponry upon the two remaining individuals. Airpower had been alerted and the exact coordinates were given to lay waste to these intruders who remained standing.

Finally, Paraffin knew it was his time. With the last of his remaining energy, he turned and bid a fond adieu to his fallen comrade, Skeeter, and his cousin, Junior Jr. III.

"Farewell, my good man. Do as I have instructed you and all will be well. Have faith, my friend. I love you."

And with that, a great metamorphosis began to transpire. There was a loud humming sound, as if a switch to a massive electrical current had been flipped. Sparks crackling with bolts of lightning and static electricity fired off inside Paraffin's protective bubble shield. All electrical equipment used by the military failed to work and completely shut down. Rifles wouldn't fire, cannons wouldn't launch, and the aircraft hovering in the skies fell and faltered to the ground. The earth trembled and wavered, and the ground rippled, as if a large pebble had been tossed into a pond. The earth started to crack open. The air turned into a tyrant, and a cyclone rose up out of a huge opening, a massive crevasse leading into the depths of the Earth's core.

Paraffin lowered his arms and pulled them into the sleeves of his robe. The blood evaporated from his already-translucent skin. He began to spasm and quiver. Light shot out from every pore in his body, similar to a mighty river springing free from the rocks of a crumbling dam. Junior Jr. and every soldier in the field were forced to shield their eyes from the light. When it was safe for the others to peer out once again, Paraffin stood in a new celestial body. He was solid blue from head to toe. Naked as an angel. His arms now controlled beautiful iridescent wings. When he opened them up and stretched them out wide, a kaleidoscope of colors shone from the sunlight refracting through them like holy stained-glass windows that changed their image with every flicker of the changing light.

Summoning the energy for one more grand thaumaturgy, Paraffin transmitted a message of peace psychically to each soldier, even those monitoring the situation from a far. The message was love and compassion, love over hate, to get in touch with your Twesa, the tenderness and kindness we all possess in our core self. With that stroke of truth and magic, a very large portion of the troops lost their will to fight; instead, they felt the overwhelming need to change and listen, to become part of the good, and to help rebuild the environment and the planet. They no longer wanted to fight, hate others, or force change upon preconceived enemies. Enemies which really didn't exist, but were created by rulers to villainize people against each other in their pursuit of power and wealth. Heartless leaders who try to tell people what to think, who believed in controlling the weak, successfully keeping the minions hating and fighting amongst themselves, while they rape and pillage the environment, and anyone who gets in their way.

Hypnotized by the powerful electromagnetic frequency that Paraffin projected, most of the soldiers changed in a powerfully emotional way. They instantly saw the futile nature of their hateful ways, but some did not react in a positive fashion. The soldiers who didn't have a change of heart fell into the gargantuan crevasse that opened up in the desert floor. Similar to Moses and the Red Sea or Dante's "Inferno", all the evil doers were swallowed up into the vast, bottomless gorge. Weapons, tanks, and planes tumbled over and into the grand canyon of the abyss. When all was finished, the opening closed, followed by the smell of death and sulfur. It left behind fresh air and the faint, sweet scent of flowers and honeysuckle, as though nothing bad had ever happened. Like no injustices were ever done.

Although Paraffin's wings were a kaleidoscope of beauty, his face showed the obvious wear of time, centuries worth –

and on two different planes of existence. Crossing the barriers of space and time, now with this last miracle, the celestial ancient prodigy was ready to make one final transition.

With the last morsel of strength he could muster, Paraffin turned and said to Junior Jr., "You're going to be okay. Have faith. People can change. Mankind as a whole can evolve. I know the division and the hatred right now is possibly greater than it's ever been before, but we can survive this. There are enough people who want to do good things for the right reasons, and we can get through this. Stay positive. If they control your mind, they win. Don't lose faith. Lead with love and compassion, kindness and understanding."

"Thank you, kind sir," Junior Jr. III replied, tears welling up in his eye sockets.

"There is a concept from the ancient yoga sutras of Patanjali. Sutra 235 states, 'In the presence of one firmly established in non-violence, all hostilities cease. When you choose to live by the vow of Ahimsa, or non-violence, it creates a ripple effect of non-violence that affects the whole world.'"

"I love you, man. Thank you for helping me be a better person."

"Thank you. Remember the things I've spoken of. Trust your instincts and follow your heart. The whole universe is being played out in you. You are infinite. There has never been a time when we did not exist, nor is there a future where we shall cease to be."

With those words, Paraffin's eyes rolled back into his

head. Static electricity crackled and sparks flew. With each pop and hum, as if a cosmic invisible generator was in control, Paraffin's feet and body lifted off the ground, delicately floating above everyone. His body hovered over the area, where just a short time earlier, it had opened up and swallowed evil doers into the Earth's core. Little balls of light, thousands of them, tiny specks of light, began to gravitate toward his body, attaching themselves to him like minnows nibbling on a crust of bread. Soon, he was covered in dots of light…until all at once, like a cosmic dandelion in a strong breeze, the particles of light turned to a golden dust that evaporated into the morning sunshine.

CHAPTER THIRTY-TWO

Stunned and in disbelief, the soldiers who survived began to chatter.

"It's a miracle," one soldier said.

"I can't believe what I just saw," admitted another.

There was much hubbub all about. Even Junior Jr. was stunned, in disbelief at what he had just witnessed. With all the commotion, Skeeter's condition had barely been noticed by Junior Jr., who now took in the full scope of the situation. Kneeling next to his fallen kinfolk, Junior Jr.'s eyes welled up as tears dripped down his face. He gently touched Skeeter's cheek with the back of his hand.

Skeeter flinched, pushed back, and hollered, "Oh, shit!

What are you doing? Get away from me!"

"Ahh, hell!" Junior Jr. screamed. "You scared me. I thought you's dead!"

"What? Hell, no! I'm not dead. What happened to me? What happened here? The last thing I remember is we were walking up on these fellas, and it was a beautiful day. I don't remember shit after that. What happened? Where's the spaceman?"

"Oh, Skeeter. You're alive, you're alive! I could just kiss you!"

"Well, don't kiss me 'cause I'd rather be dead *and* your breath stinks. What happened?"

Junior Jr. explained to Skeeter what had happened. A young soldier came over and brought water to each of them. Everyone gathered around the spot where the earth had opened up just moments earlier. Skeeter and Junior Jr. explained as best they could what was at stake. A psychic transmission to Mars to teleport a special substance available only on Mars was going to enable mankind to heal the damage to Earth at a quantum pace.

"Like a needle on a record player, this special form of carbon nitride will work like a conduit, enabling the technology being developed by a special group of scientists to project into the atmosphere a unique frequency combination that will clear and heal the Earth's atmosphere," Junior Jr. explained to them. Paraffin had given Junior Jr. this information during a brief moment of hypnosis in the cave.

Back at The Crystal City, Ryder, Crystal, Grace, and the

team of scientists were assembling and tuning the mirror on a new reflective telescope receiver. It was a unique telescope that they had just finished building, the first of its kind. A telescope that could not only look out into the sky, but could also send and receive information, similar to a giant megaphone. The team was preparing to broadcast a healing vibrational frequency that would cleanse the atmosphere, eventually seeping into the earth and water system, ridding it of poison and pollutants while refortifying its natural system with the ingredients it needed to be healthy and clean again. If all goes as calculated, this process would enable humans around the world to have fresh air, clean water, and food again. No longer will there be a need for starvation pills or water tablets to purify water into a thick, lumpy oatmeal substance.

Nora was foraging the forest, harvesting plants for a potion to go with the incantation she had written, blessing the team's efforts. The colonies on Mars and the team on Earth completed many dry runs, sending items of little importance back and forth safely before transporting the quantities of Herculean barometric carbon nitride needed to complete the special ray gun that would reverse global warming and heal the atmosphere. If the weather conditions remained favorable, it was possible the team would attempt the first firing of the special frequency spectrum ray gun that afternoon.

"The frequency combinations and the equation written by Noah Billingsworth were a special series of harmonics inaudible to the human ear," Ryder explained. "Not because the notes are too high or too low for our hearing; the notes are frequencies in between the frequencies that we can already hear. Just as there are dimensions dividing other dimensions of our plane of existence. Like if two universes were different pieces of graph paper, each crossing each other's existence, but neither one can see the other, these notes transmitted are in between the frequencies that we have the ability to hear."

The excitement was palpable. The team was brimming with pride and nervousness as they prepared for the first launch and firing of the Crystal Grace Irradiation Frequency Spectrum Ray Gun. Crystal and Grace were the two prominent architects for the concept and design of the Irradiation Frequency Spectrum Ray Gun, and the committee of scientists agreed that their names should be included in the naming of this planet-saving device.

After several days of postponements due to unfavorable weather, at last, the day arrived, a perfect 68°F morning with clear skies and little wind. The coordinates were set, and the Crystal Grace Irradiation Frequency Spectrum Ray Gun shot a beam of energy – a combination of neurons and protons tuned to a specific harmonic frequency, inaudible to any living creature on Earth – into the vortex of the atmosphere. The team erupted into a collective outpouring of awes and cheers. Emotions spilled over with ecstasy and satisfaction. Tears flowed, and spontaneous speeches and shout-outs to each other were given. Everyone felt relief from years of struggling to survive, as well as the hard work and preparation of building this unique device. The team gathered itself as the Crystal Grace Irradiation Frequency Spectrum Ray Gun was re-aimed and refocused into 12 more coordinates, interjecting its therapeutic properties into the atmosphere.

The healing had begun.

Once things took effect, the plan was to build and materialize more of the Crystal Grace Irradiation Frequency Spectrum Ray Guns to other countries and continents around the world, and to share the schematics and blueprints needed to build this miraculous invention.

Celebrations were well-deserved. The team gave itself a party that evening, with much love and merriment shared amongst one another. The celebrations, however, were short-lived, as news arrived the following morning that Queen Daffodil and her remaining forces were on the rise. The Queen and her evil forces were seizing and torturing anyone perceived to be undermining her efforts. If she felt they posed a threat in any fashion, these individuals were executed.

CHAPTER THIRTY-THREE

Using psychic solar radio communication with Skeeter and Junior Jr. III, the team of scientists at The Crystal City determined their location and set out to find the two cousins. They were also able to surmise that the pair had witnessed a fantastic miracle performed by Paraffin, a final offering for his host planet, the place he called home for the last 12 centuries. Before the celestial being transcended into another realm of existence, Paraffin transformed and shifted an entire army's perspective, changing their will to kill and conquer into a desire to help and heal mankind. The tricky part was how to conquer the mind of Queen Daffodil and the soldiers who still followed her whims and orders.

Skeeter and Junior Jr. III had no military training. They never led anyone or anybody anywhere or into anything before in their lives. Yet, the officers in charge of the 2,800 troops transformed by Paraffin agreed to follow them and do as they saw fit. Ryder, Nora, Crystal, Grace, and the team of scientists headed by Orville and Norman Poff joined forces at a fork in a ravine formed by two large rivers converging inside a 300-foot gorge. The newly converted army led by Skeeter and Junior Jr. III met up with the group led by Ryder and Nora, along with Crystal and Grace and the team of scientists. Ryder, being the only one who had recently traveled the entire distance to the countryside near Queen Daffodil's lair, became the lead scout. Nora foraged the trailhead while looking out for any dangers that may await them on their journey.

Before they began their pursuit, Nora took a potion she made from wild truffles and mushrooms, and fell into a trance. Her thoughts turned to patterns, shapes of petals, and then a lotus morphed into the head of a tiger. The tiger's mouth opened wide enough for Nora to fall inside, passing the animal's giant teeth and into the dark void of its chasm. There she lay in darkness, resting on a mucus-lined floor of what she believed to be the inside of this giant tiger's stomach. She fell asleep and drifted off into a dream – a dream inside a dream. And inside this dream, a voice came to her and posed a question, "Would you rather fight to survive, or would you rather love to survive?"

Nora thought to herself, *"Even though I'm willing to fight to survive if I had to, I would much rather love to survive."* Survive on love rather than surviving on hate and the conditioned fighting and wars that so many people had been born into. They had lived with war their entire lives; it was all that they knew.

With this realization, the darkness turned to light. She woke up inside the tiger, stood up out of the mucus, and materialized back into existence. She first whispered her thoughts to Ryder. Then she gathered everyone in the team. Skeeter, Junior Jr., the newly converted officers who were the former soldiers from The Queen's brigade, the team of scientists, Crystal, and Grace listened intently as Nora explained to them what she saw in her vision.

"We need to stop the violence. We cannot expect to kill off all of our enemies. We must counter their aggression with kindness and understanding. We'll have to try and overpower The Queen's psychic abilities to see if we can touch her tender heart…if she has one. Some people are pure evil and psychotic; the possibility to reach her on any kind of empathetic level may not exist. But, if we can change the minds of the rest of her followers, maybe we can reduce her powers. There is proof that with the energy and powers possessed by a being such as Queen Daffodil, if we can reduce the energy other people are feeding her, we can actually tremendously diminish her physical and psychic abilities."

"If we focus our thoughts like beams of light, we can send our message similar to the way we sent the messages to the colonies on Mars. Still, we must be prepared to defend ourselves if necessary. If under direct physical attack, we must either fight back, or try to run away and live to fight another day."

"We're here to protect you if your peaceful mind control fails to stop them," Colonel Wallerstein stated. Colonel Wallerstein was the highest-ranking officer among the recently converted troops.

They moved out under the cover of darkness. Riding on a newly refurbished bike, Ryder scouted the trail ahead of the others with Nora, who like a satellite, circled around the area, tuning in for any vibrations of danger. After four nights of traveling, they arrived at a flange in the terrain. Beyond that, about a quarter of a mile, was a huge berm then the remains of a burnt-out forest destroyed from counterattacks by rebels against The Queen. Hiding and observing from a distance, the team formulated a plan.

"Below that berm," Ryder explained, "there's an entrance to The Queen's lair. If she doesn't already know we're here, I'm sure she'll figure it out soon enough."

Colonel Wallerstein began giving orders. "Dolan, you and Sergeant Asch take your men and go to the rear to make sure we're not being followed. Kleinman, take some men and keep a watch overlooking the ridge to the southwest. Gentry, you and Sanders take your platoons to the right flank overlooking that dome of earth to the east. Whatever you do, don't make any noise and under no circumstances fire your weapons unless we're under direct attack. We are on a mission of peace. Lieutenant Steinberg, I need your expertise here with me. Keep an eye on the thermal radar shield and tell me at once if the signals dip into the 78th quadrant or show any signs of movement."

The team dug into their surroundings. Telepathic invisible shields were connected in an attempt to repel any psychic detection from Queen Daffodil and her remaining forces. Observation posts were set up on the perimeters of the camp. There was very little movement. No patrols guarded the area around the hidden entrance to The Queen's underground palace.

"We may not have enough power to hold up our shields from detection by The Queen for very long," Crystal told them.

Colonel Wallerstein turned to Skeeter and said, "With your permission, I think I should send out three or four small patrols to search the outlying areas of the perimeter."

Skeeter rubbed his horn as he contemplated the colonel's words, puzzled that he would ask him for permission to do anything.

"That's a good idea," Grace replied. "If we can engage with only a few numbers of soldiers at a time, it will be to our advantage. It'll be much easier to sway the perspective of a smaller group rather than the whole of the remaining army at once."

Ryder agreed. "It's true. These soldiers have families and they're probably tired of the fighting, coupled with the poor conditions they're forced to live in. Surely they're concerned with their own family's needs and the lack of clean water and healthy food left on the planet. If we can show them that we have a solution, perhaps we can get them to stop fighting."

"The overwhelming greed of Queen Daffodil must be

stopped!" Crystal demanded.

"People have free will, so there'll be some who won't change. But just as Paraffin's world was able to evolve many centuries ago, we can evolve, too. We can change. The majority of humans are good and would rather work in harmony with one another than to be in conflict with each other. If we don't kill it, we can take care of it. There are enough resources on the planet for everyone to survive and to live well. However, we must take care of what we have, the Earth, and each other," stated Nora.

"Eradicate greed, nurture kindness and empathy, and live in harmony with one another and our surroundings. Why does it have to be so difficult?" Ryder asked.

"The human condition is complicated," Grace answered. "We must lead with kindness and understanding in order to evolve. If we can engage our aggressors – those with hateful and treacherous goals and opinions – and not retaliate with aggression, we will do more good than harm."

As the prominent leader of her team, Crystal took charge directing the soldiers. "Colonel Wallerstein, you divide your troops as you see fit. Please engage anyone you encounter peacefully. Hopefully, you won't have to use any weaponry."

Colonel Wallerstein began sending his men out on patrol. "Knutson, you and Foxworthy take patrols westward about half a click from the berm. Steinberg, I'm going to need you to track any temperature changes on your thermal radar. Alert me at once if there's even the slightest detection of movement or manifestations."

Colonel Wallerstein continued organizing and directing

the troops while the team of scientists continued monitoring their own equipment and formulating a plan to use a smaller version of the Crystal Grace Irradiation Frequency Spectrum Ray Gun.

Crystal explained, "If we can create a beam of light containing proponents and the attributes of a magnet, we can disarm the soldiers of any weapons. Grace and I haven't fully tested the equation we've formulated, but we're close enough to having it ready to give it a whirl. We'll have to hope that our calculations are correct. If we engage a reasonable number of soldiers at once, we should be able to disarm any patrol we encounter. Once we disarm them, Nora can work with her telepathy to tap into and influence their Tsewa."

"What is Tsewa?" Colonel Wallerstein inquired.

"Tsewa is from the ancient Tibetan Buddhism teachings. It's the most essential form of enlightenment and refers to our open hearts," Crystal explained.

Colonel Wallerstein, along with the help of Lieutenant Steinberg and his men, started to disperse. Ryder, Nora, Skeeter, and Junior Jr. set out directly toward the middle of the berm leading to the forest. The cloaking devices were engaged on Ryder's bicycle and helmet, keeping them protected from being detected by The Queen's psychic radar. One by one, small parties of Queen Daffodil's troops were detected, hidden, camouflaged by their own cloaking devices, guarding the protected area leading to the secret entrance of her underground palace. The smaller versions of the Crystal Grace Irradiation Frequency Spectrum Ray Guns were used with much success, firing at the hidden troops, and disabling them and their weapons. Most of The Queen's soldiers required little telepathy or reasoning to surrender, quickly giving in to the positive vibrations and the hope of having a better future. Instead of fighting, many of the soldiers finally surrendered with the dream of living peacefully, rather than continuing to live in the vile conditions they were subjected to working under The Queen's regime. Some, however, were not able to be subdued, so they either fled to alert their superiors, or charged and fought Wallerstein and his soldiers. Most of these soldiers were fearful of The Queen's retaliation and what she would do to their families if they were to give up fighting. Those that did resist fought valiantly, yet died in vain. Soldiers full of anger and hate fell, like any creature unable to adapt to change, instantly becoming extinct. Now, they tasted the fruits of death – fruits they had served onto countless others – as they perished in the field.

The quartet, protected by Ryder's cloaking device, could have been mistaken for some friends on a lovely stroll through the woods, if not for the perilous life-and-death situation they faced with the violent fighting occurring around them. Their nerves and senses were on high alert from the impending danger. Queen Daffodil was now aware of the goings-on of the team and the newly converted soldiers of peace.

Ryder's bike was equipped with a radar device that warned them as they neared the berm on the edge of the forest. The newly refurbished bicycle was also well-equipped with a smaller version of the Crystal Grace Irradiation Frequency Spectrum Ray Gun. It had several functions and settings that varied in the ability to immobilize threats ranging from mild temporary paralysis to complete annihilation. It could also be set to restorative energy that was capable of healing fractures and wounds in nature and people.

"Why are you stopping? What's chur gizmo say there?" Junior Jr. wanted to know.

"There's something in front of us. It looks like there's other soldiers starting to close in on us…probably The Queen's guards. They must be under the protection of some sort of cloaking device as well. I don't think they can see us, but they must be able to detect our energy on some level. I'm afraid they know we're here. Even if they aren't able to pinpoint exactly where we are, they're on to us. Don't be alarmed, but we appear to be greatly outnumbered."

"Everybody, breathe. Stay focused and calm," Nora told them. "Ryder's shield is holding strong. I have a spell I'm going to perform. Ryder, now would be a good time to set the CGIRG Mini to the suspended animation setting. If we can contain most of the soldiers surrounding us, we can hopefully control the situation without killing anyone."

"We need to convey the message that we're not here to fight them, but that we're one of them," Skeeter said.

"That's right," Junior Jr. added.

"We're liable to be their kinfolk," Skeeter continued, Junior Jr. nodding in agreement. "We all have families and want to do the best for our children and elders. Now, I finally see how so much of the division amongst everyone was generated by Queen Daffodil in her efforts to hoard wealth, power, and control. I want to help spread the message of kindness, love, and peace."

Nora began reciting an incantation. Ryder knew that in order to use the CGIRG Mini, they would need to disengage the cloaking shield protecting them from being detected. Nora opened her eyes and stopped her recitation.

"Okay, it's time we make our move," she stated.

"What do you want us to do?" Junior Jr. asked.

"I need you and Skeeter to show no fear, keep your thoughts razor-focused on kindness and empathy toward these soldiers."

Junior Jr. agreed and said, "I remember what Paraffin told me. Stay positive, if they control your mind, they win."

"That's right" Nora said. "We mustn't seem scared or weak. We shouldn't act aggressively either. We must pose no threat. In order to hold them in a state of suspended animation, our thoughts must be pure of intention for my spell to work. If we can get them to feel safe, acknowledging their true feelings in this hypnotic state and releasing their fears, perhaps we can convince them to lay down their arms. Recently, the numbers of her followers have been greatly diminished and hopefully more will follow suit."

Ryder spoke up, "Queen Daffodil is going to be the toughest one to overcome."

"If we can diminish her forces, the power she gets from those who believe in her, that will take away her energy. That will be our only hope," Nora responded.

"I hope I don't have to hurt no one. I ain't never kilt another body before, and I don't want to start now," Skeeter said reluctantly. "Even if it's in self-defense, I don't wanna hurt nobody."

Skeeter began to get a little queasy. He stroked the felt on his horn for comfort. Junior Jr. put his big hand on Skeeter's back. His fat fingers wrapped easily around the boney collarbone bridging Skeeter's skinny neck with the scrawny ball of his shoulder.

"Don't worry, Skeeter." Junior Jr. said. "Ryder and Nora know what they're doing. I'll look out for ya. Don't choo worry."

"Yes, no need to worry," Nora confirmed. "Ryder, do you have a pretty good idea of the location of each of the soldiers circling around us?"

"Yes. Even though my radar might not have their precise location, the margin of error is close enough to allow the suspended animation beam to work accurately."

"Okay, is everybody ready?"

Everyone looked at each other and nodded affirmatively.

"Ryder, when you disengage the cloaking device, start zapping every area you detect with the energy field. When they become zapped with the ray gun, their cloaking devices will shut down and they will no longer be invisible. Are you ready?"

"Let's do this!" Junior Jr. exclaimed, clapping his hands and rubbing them together enthusiastically.

Ryder took note of the closest energy field, and then the next, and so on. Flipping the switch and turning off the cloaking device, Ryder enabled the CGIRG Mini to fire a laser beam of energy, sending soldiers – one after the other – floating in a suspended animation, free of fears, worries, aggression, or biases. Just their true, inherent, innocent beings floated above the ground. Some of the soldiers resisted, fighting back and firing at the quartet before Ryder zapped them with the ray gun.

The quartet split up and took cover. Nora worked her magic telepathy, communicating with the soldiers in suspended animation, tapping into their souls and relating to them as sentient beings, and in turn, getting them to relate to all humans as sentient beings, too. Some continued to resist, but many were more than relieved to see a way out of the grip of Queen Daffodil's evil regime. Most of the soldiers were only fighting out of fear – the fear and the control that The Queen held over their lives and the safety of their families. Much of The Queen's psychic powers were fueled by the will and energy that her minions gave her. When more people quit believing in her, it weakened her psychic powers.

Bullets whizzed all around them. Skeeter, Junior Jr., Nora, and Ryder took cover hiding amongst the terrain. Ryder continued to keep an eye on the radar screen to try to locate energy fields, and used the other eye to aim and fire the ray gun. Nora continued with her telepathy as Skeeter and Junior Jr. tried to remain confident while hiding and thinking positive thoughts.

Queen Daffodil knew that if more of her army were to defect, it not only would weaken the numbers to fight for her, but it would also weaken her psychic powers. The time had come for Queen Daffodil to materialize, taking matters into her own hands. The skies darkened. Thunder clouds opened up, shooting fire and lightning across the horizon, followed by a sheet of hailstones and smoke. It was a juxtaposition of weather. The smell of sulfur permeated the region to the extent that nausea and vomiting affected those who inhaled it. The stench and weather parted as Queen Daffodil appeared before Ryder and the others. She lifted the four of them out of their individual hiding places with torches that shot from her fingers, placing them on the ground in front of her.

"Why do you wish to destroy me?" she bellowed.

"We don't wish to destroy you," Ryder answered. "We only wish to help all of mankind and our planet."

"We want to help, not harm," said Skeeter.

"Poppycock!" The Queen hollered. She looked at Skeeter and said, "What happened to you? Where did you get that horn? It looks like an allergic reaction of a subharmonic frequency beam. I only know of one or two beings that possess the ability to perform such a thing, and I know one of them no longer exists. How would you all like to be turned into space dust like your friend, Paraffin?"

"Paraffin chose to transcend. By doing so, he convinced a large portion of your army to give up fighting and to put their energy and skills into healthier, positive activities. Paraffin taught us many things," Ryder said.

"Yeah, and those he didn't influence fell into the chasm of hell!" barked The Queen. "You people are going to have to pay for that. I'm going to enjoy killing each and every one of you!"

Queen Daffodil hit Nora first with a beam of energy dead center in her chest. The blast took her breath away, knocking her unconscious and nearly killing her. Bullets continued to zip past the heads of everyone, making it difficult for Skeeter and Junior Jr. to not flinch or take cover. The Queen threw a ball of energy, like a cosmic soap bubble, that engulfed Skeeter and Junior Jr., rendering them powerless as they were lifted and floated off the ground. Skeeter scampered on his hands and feet, as if he was trapped in a giant hamster ball, but it did nothing to alleviate their situation. He tried puncturing the cosmic soap bubble with his horn, but it did no good. It only repelled his head backwards, causing him to fall on his butt, bouncing gingerly, like he was on a trampoline.

"It's no use," Junior Jr. said. "We're trapped…at least for the time being."

Queen Daffodil locked her gaze onto Ryder and stated, "It's you I'm most interested in. You're the one I hold the most responsible for the weakening of my powers and my empire. It's you who came into contact with my arch nemesis, Noah Billingsworth."

She repeated her words and clicked her tongue on the roof of her mouth before continuing, "Noah Billingsworth, that little fat dumpling of a man, is the root of my anguish. That little fucker has cracked the code. Oh, there were others at play. The scientist in that God-blasted Crystal City, which I could never quite locate, that damn celestial being, Paraffin, and so many others. But now you…you are high on my list of those I look forward to torturing and killing."

With each word, Queen Daffodil found it harder and harder to concentrate. Every soldier and person who now realized they no longer had to live under her spell converted their energy and relinquished their beliefs in The Queen. This weakened her psychic powers exponentially. Still, she held these four under a spell and hoped to regain the strength to locate and destroy Noah Billingsworth and his cryogenic suspended animation chamber.

The Queen's eyes rested on Ryder. Her maniacal laughter broke through the brief silence like thunder before a storm. She cried, "I plan to kill you and your little friends, too! But first, I'm going to suck out every last drop of matter from your brain, giving me the knowledge and information of Noah Billingsworth and his whereabouts, as well as the knowledge and information he gave you. I will destroy him!"

Ryder feared the worst and wondered if it was time to flip the switch on the bicycle's laser to zap The Queen and destroy her. Would that even be possible? Was there time to set the ray gun to incinerate and kill The Queen? Would it be for the best to permanently eradicate Queen Daffodil? So many thoughts simultaneously raced through Ryder's head, making it hard to focus.

The Queen, however, wasn't done yet and could sense something was wrong. She noticed Ryder's thoughts and focus on the bicycle. Her powers were weakening, but she still had plenty of strength to seize the bike, separating it away from Ryder. The Queen averted her attention to the bicycle. Although her powers continued to weaken, she had enough energy left in her to melt the bike right before their eyes. The bicycle crumpled and shriveled into a disfigured wad, completely enveloping itself. Like a piece of yarn or strip of plastic in a fiery blaze, it crinkled into itself before turning into a single flame that burned into a tiny puff of smoke. It was as if a loved one had been executed right in front of everyone to witness. Helpless to do anything about it, Ryder collapsed to the ground.

Queen Daffodil, full of pride and pleasure, roared with maniacal laughter. Her joy knew no limit and she shook uncontrollably with cachinnation. Unable to contain herself, she lost her focus. With her guard down, she was unaware of a vengeful turncoat wielding a saber. Marcus Junius was once a devout soldier for Queen Daffodil. He had fought valiantly for The Queen, conquering nations and states, helping her to accumulate mass fortunes and wealth. He had believed that what he was doing was for the good of himself and others. However, he had recently become disillusioned, but had no means of recourse and was not able to retaliate until now. He stood with the razor-sharp saber that was more than capable of slicing off the demon's head. Easier than slicing through butter or a piece of fruit.

News was already traveling around the globe that The Queen was falling. More countries and individuals worldwide began to take to the streets in ecstasy with the news of her demise. Those who believed in her, afraid to stand up to her perceived strength, no longer wanted to follow her evil ways. Nations afraid of her wrath and retaliation no longer feared her; they vowed to stand up for peace, taking a more humane approach in caring for its citizens. With each person who felt the relief of true freedom and equanimity, The Queen's psychic powers and physical strength were weakening. Her powers were getting zapped, diminishing incrementally with each passing moment.

"Don't move," Marcus Junius demanded. He knew The Queen's powers were weakening. "I used to believe that I was doing good for you – that all the peasants we were dominating and controlling were actually inferior to us. I believed that we were better than them and that we were somehow doing them a favor. I believed that we deserved the riches we stole and that we would be smiled upon by the grace of God, that we would live rich and rewarding lives. What I came to realize was that your greed and psychotic desires were all that mattered to you. You didn't care about those of us who were doing your bidding. I saw loyal followers of yours being slaughtered by you, simply for sport. If you thought they slighted you in any way, you'd torture and kill them *and* their families. You never took care of me or my family, and what's even worse, is now I've realized the evil and trauma I have inflicted on others. How I could do that and think it was okay, I don't know. I feel as though nothing can redeem me. But one small thing I can do to try to pay pittance toward the horrible things I've done, is rid you of this planet."

"No don't!" Ryder shouted.

"Why would you say that?" Marcus Junius asked. "I intend to slice the head off of the serpent. Is it not better to rid the world of her vile, poisonous influence and power?

Think back through history. Would it not have been better if an assassin had taken out those who would come into power and kill millions of people they deemed unworthy? If we could prevent those things from happening, wouldn't that be better? If you could save millions of lives by killing just one evil person, wouldn't that be better? For the good of all humans?"

Light gleamed off the saber that Marcus Junius held at the ready, firmly in both hands. Queen Daffodil, dizzy and lightheaded from the loss of thousands, then millions of followers and believers, became anemic and weak, as if in a bloodletting.

Ryder responded, "The easy answer would seem to be yes. But who are we to say who should live and who should die? There's probably no way to completely eradicate the bad behavior of people, but I feel like we can greatly reduce it by leading by example. I'm not sure if killing the bad ones will make it all go away. There's bound to still be people who will follow or act as Queen Daffodil has done. If we kill her, she may become a martyr or a symbol of what she represented to those who still believe in her. There are many who only think they should believe in her. The more we quit making it okay to be like her, perhaps we can shift everyone's perspective…and without the use of hypnosis or magic. People, leaders, and rulers should be doing the right thing because it's the right thing to do."

Parts of Queen Daffodil's forces were closing in, not

giving up. Colonel Wallerstein and his men were forced to return fire. They were beginning to sustain heavy losses. Fortunately, with the heroic efforts of recon specialist Lieutenant Pablo Steinberg, the group was able to retaliate. Steinberg led a charge against a foe that greatly outnumbered his patrol. He saved countless lives by disemboweling an entire regiment, including infantry, tanks, and artillery, with a series of high-volume explosives. Exploding tanks set forth a sonic boom, echoing and shaking the ground. Those standing fell.

Queen Daffodil's concentration was broken. No longer able to control her thoughts, she dropped the cosmic bubble containing Skeeter and Junior Jr., plummeting them to the ground. With her forces fighting back and no longer needing to concentrate on the soap bubble holding Skeeter and Junior Jr., Queen Daffodil began regaining some of her strength and power. Her ears were ringing, her vision slightly blurred. She tossed her head back and forth, trying to clear her senses as she prepared to retaliate. Marcus Junius stood up and retrieved his sword, which fell from his hands when the explosion occurred that knocked him to the ground. Queen Daffodil's troops were closing in on Colonel Wallerstein, Lieutenant Steinberg and the others.

The Queen rubbed her head and chuckled, "You fool! You could've finished me off, but now I'll live to fight another day."

In spite of the efforts of the converted army led by Colonel Wallerstein, The Queen's forces were not yet done. Junius raised his sword and charged The Queen. She held up her hand and stopped the turncoat in his tracks.

"You cannot harm me now, you pathetic fool! Your emotions make you a weakling."

She broke out into another maniacal cackle; this time, however, she did not lose control of herself. In the commotion, Nora, unnoticed by the others, came to. She was beginning to stir and regain her strength. Skeeter and Junior Jr. shook off the fall and were helping the others to their feet. Soldiers with The Queen's guard were rushing forward. Ryder, seeing Junius in the grips of Queen Daffodil's powers and wanting to disarm the situation, instantly hurried over to help. A marksman with The Queen's guard saw this impending attack on Queen Daffodil and fired, aiming directly for the kill. In the marksman's hurry, his first two shots missed the target, but homing in more carefully, the third shot was not to miss.

Skeeter and Junior Jr. watched the situation unfold. Flying over as fast as possible, Skeeter was determined to help. It was as if the world started spinning in slow motion. Skeeter leapt to render aid and save his friend from death. Things moved so slowly. It seemed as though he was able to run circles around the incoming bullets. He could see the smoke from the gun and the pointy end of the bullet, shining in the light as it spun in a circle, projecting through the atmosphere and rocketing toward Ryder. He could tell by the slow-motion flight of the first round that the bullet was way in front of its target. He was close enough to the second round that he felt like he was a nanosecond away from snatching it out of the air with his very grip. By the third shot, though, Skeeter was able to get a bead on the bullet. He was neck and neck with it, determined and sure he could beat the projectile to its destination. While everything was still moving in ultra slow motion, Skeeter jumped and grabbed Ryder's shoulders so that the bullet did not hit its target, but flew into the softness of Skeeter's heart instead.

As soon as the bullet went into his chest, the world returned to its normal pace. Gravity worked. Skeeter fell fast back down to Earth.

CHAPTER THIRTY-FOUR

The converted soldiers of peace and the army for The People's People had regrouped, and they were preparing an onslaught of The Queen's guards and what remained of her army. Queen Daffodil knew her resources were tapped. She sent out a call to retreat.

Before turning to leave, she said, "You can't do away with me or people like me. If you kill me, somebody else will step in and fill the void. Good can't outdo evil, but evil can always outdo good."

She looked ill, struggling to breathe as she spoke the wretched words.

"No, you're wrong!" Ryder said. "There may always be a

yin and yang with good and evil, love and hate, but I do believe that there's more of us who believe that good can overcome evil or anything else, for that matter. There are more people who believe in that than those who don't. Just look at what's happening to you. As more and more people stop believing in you and stop following you, you're losing your powers before our very eyes. I do think we can change the world if we just keep striving for peace and justice for everyone. Treat everybody equally with kindness and love. That's what the world needs."

Using the last bits of magic powers she had at her disposal, Queen Daffodil conjured a spell. Waving her arms and hands in fast, repetitive motions in front of her face and torso, she disappeared into a splash of light that vanished as quickly as it appeared.

Junior Jr. and Nora barely took notice as they rushed to Skeeter. He lay there, his eyes open. He sputtered and coughed as globs of blood came out of his mouth.

Skeeter chuckled and said, "Damn thing got me."

Nora laid her hands on him, summoning what powers she could to save poor Skeeter, but there was nothing she could do.

"It's okay, y'all. Don't be sad for me. It's for the greater good that it happened this way."

"Don't say that, Skeeter! You deserve to live as much as me. You saved my life," Ryder said.

"No, really. I'm just paying you back. You and Paraffin saved my life by teaching me a different way of living."

Skeeter sputtered and stopped talking to cough up a little

more blood. Junior Jr. was weeping. He put his hands on his friend and relative.

"You taught me a better outlook for life and humanity," Skeeter said. He reached up to touch his horn. "I just wanted to help."

And with those last words, Skeeter transitioned over into another existence, leaving behind his body with a horn.

With the aid of Colonel Wallerstein, Lieutenant Steinberg, and their men, Ryder, Nora, and Junior Jr. took Skeeter's body back to where Paraffin parted this world. The same place where the earth opened up and swallowed The Queen's army. The trip was much shorter this time since they didn't have to travel in secrecy. It was a sunny day with pleasant temperatures. They picked a lush area on top of the hill overlooking the meadow where Paraffin performed his miracle. Saying prayers and sharing stories, they held a ceremony and laid Skeeter to rest under an olive tree.

Many years later, this area became a hub for a new civilization – one that had learned to live in peace with one another. There was a massive interstellar and transglobal transportation hub named after the wise celestial being, Paraffin.

Paraffin Station was a new Mecca for travelers far and wide. It was able to accommodate the gathering needs of locals, with parks, restaurants, and meditative houses of worship, all serving as peaceful gathering places for the local and world community.

Crystal and Grace returned home to The Crystal City and continued their work in the advancement of scientific technologies. The irradiation ray gun that bore their names continued to be used in the healing of the planet's atmosphere and water. Mankind and technology began to flourish. More and more people started to evolve, working in conjunction with one another, realizing that if one person is doing poorly, it will affect everyone. With enough individuals doing poorly, eventually all beings will be doing poorly; but if each and every individual is doing well, then everyone is doing well. The arm can't do its job if the foot has a disease. It's the same with each person, plant, and molecule on the planet – if one part is doing poorly, it affects everyone.

Queen Daffodil never rose to the power she once had. Eventually, more and more of her followers quit believing in her, further diminishing her ability to rule. Over time, her henchmen were caught and sentenced to imprisonment. Queen Daffodil herself was never captured or held accountable in a court of law, but her followers turned on her, one by one. She betrayed each and every one of them, never rendering aid or support to any of them when they needed it. The wealth she acquired from decades of plunder was lost. Unable to enjoy the fruits of her waning years, she died penniless, miserable, and alone, her body overcome with the slow and painful death of pancreatic cancer, coupled with lymphoma, tuberculosis, and necrotizing fasciitis, a flesh-eating bacterium she contracted from living in a dank cave on a remote sandbar in a desolate, hot, and humid mosquito-infested island in the middle of nowhere.

Ryder and Nora stayed together and were married in a

modest ceremony performed by Claire the Clairvoyant. Unable to have children, Ryder and Nora adopted many orphans and settled down in the old-growth forest of Nora's ancestors. Ryder opened a bicycle shop and Nora was the community's medicine woman and shamanic healer. They remained close and stayed in touch with Crystal and Grace, taking turns hosting each other for the holidays.

Norman and Orville Poff developed a technology that freed Noah Billingsworth from his cryogenic suspended animation chamber, which allowed him, the Moynihans, and the others to move back and forth into the current realm of existence.

Colonel Wallerstein and Lieutenant Pablo Steinberg ran for office and became the first president and vice president of the newly reformed United States of America. Steinberg won the nomination and picked his former commander as his running mate. They ran on a platform of compassion and peace and warned against the dangers of the military-industrial complex.

With the passing of time, decades turned into half-centuries, which turned into centennials and beyond. Mankind evolved into a more sophisticated animal. New governments formed that took care of its citizens. Food, water, and clean, fresh air were now the standard. Opportunities for everyone to share in the abundance that life had to offer almost eliminated the need for crime. Still, evil lurked, creeping like a sludge through the pores of goodwill, like a cancer hiding in the shadows of ignorance and hate. There were those who continued to try and manipulate the system, hoarding wealth only for themselves, but fewer and fewer people resorted to such tactics. Those who did were no longer tolerated in the global society.

Helping one another became the norm. Sayings like "Consciously choosing right actions" and "We all have the potential for enlightenment in this life" became slogans around the world. Surviving the near-total destruction of the planet and the extinction of mankind gave humans a renewed outlook on life, learning how to treat one another equally with love, compassion, and respect. Mankind evolved, learning to work and live together in peace, so everyone could prosper, survive, and take care of their own.

ACKNOWLEDGMENTS

I would like to thank the following people who have encouraged and inspired me in my quest to tell stories. It's still a learning process. I've had many inspiring teachers. Some taught me creative writing, some introduced me to great literature, while some have done both.

First and foremost, to Bob Davis, my eighth grade English teacher. You recognized my enthusiasm and pointed out to me some skills I had in describing things. You gave me the encouragement and awareness I needed, and the extra time on my assignments (which I always needed), so I could do this.

To my friend and high school English and creative writing teacher, Scott Davison. I owe you much gratitude for the things you taught me, including how to embrace life. You're still a good influence on me.

To Mrs. Williams, my English teacher my junior year of high school, for assigning me *Slaughterhouse Five* by Kurt Vonnegut, Jr. That was a life-changing experience. It opened my mind to a whole new realm of creativity in a story.

To Donna Northouse and Evan Higgins, also outstanding English teachers, who helped shape me. I appreciate the books and short stories you shared with me and the encouragement you gave me in my writing.

To my many friends and bandmates who have encouraged me, read my stories, and gave me positive feedback over the years, I thank you.

To my lifelong friend and bandmate, Kenny Withrow…Dude! We've shared so many amazing moments together. The bonds we formed at an early age are deep; you're like a blood brother to me. You're an inspiration. I'm very grateful for our time together.

To my dear friend, Edie Brickell, who has always been a trusted confidant and editor of many of my earliest short stories. You've really helped me to have faith in myself.

To another brother and lifelong bandmate, Brandon Aly. I thank you for all the fun, music, and munches we've shared together. You're a reliable friend with a tender soul and a heart of gold.

Many other close friends have read or helped me edit some of my stories over the years. You all have given me inspiration, encouragement, or (at times) a place to write. With love and gratitude, I thank you: Adina Richman,

Christina Housand Morris, Kenny Stern, Reed Easterwood, Cleve Hattersley, Wayne Sutton, Chelsey Clammer, Stacy Summers, Scott Johnson, Frank Patrick Turrentine, Brian Withrow, Kevin Dehan, David Breed, Kimble Hayes, Melissa Vance Wilson, Landis Armstrong, Kelly Higgins, Dave Moynihan, Beverly Baker, David 'Smitty' Little-Smith, Katherine Johnson, Steven Karme, Nicholas Polimenakos, Regina Findlay, Scott and Nicki Turman, Patrice Pike, Hunter Hendrickson, Kelly Ramsey Webb, Lance Webb, Christina Nelson, Gena Pelham, and The Drakes (Matt, Mike, Jorge, Ron, and Cornbread.)

I also want to thank my children who I love and adore, Elec and Livvy, and to their loving mom, Suzy Whitlock.

To my wonderful brother and sister, David Bush and Sarah Ellis. Both of you have had a profound and positive influence on my life. I've learned so much from both of you. You have supported me and encouraged me every step of the way and in everything I've ever done. Sarah, you've always been my greatest ally. I still recall the times we spent together as children and the tales I'd tell you. I would mash together *Goldilocks and The Three Bears*, *Little Red Riding Hood*, and *The Three Little Pigs* into one story, jumping around from one story to the next and always picking up where I left off with each story until all three had been told in their entirety. I think that's how I learned to jump around in time and with different places in my stories today. David, you've always been there for me when I've needed it most. You were, and still are, a protective big brother. You helped guide me in my taste of music growing up and your work ethic is admirable. I thank you both for your unconditional love and support throughout my entire life.

To my mother, Kathie Remington Poff, and my father, Bob Bush. Daddy, you were the one who influenced and encouraged me first when I worked up the courage to read you a story that I had written when we lived in Bonham. I was probably in the fourth or fifth grade. The story wasn't a school assignment, but something I wrote for fun. The story was set around the 1860s because we'd just read *The Red Badge of Courage* in school. You also gave me an excellent foundation in morals and the acceptance of others, no matter their beliefs or ideology. You also taught all your kids how to camp and inspired our love for nature and the great outdoors. And to my sweet mother, who was a schoolteacher and so deeply passionate about science and the students she taught. Her eyes lit up with the excitement of a child when she'd share her knowledge about rocks, minerals, or outer space.

I'd like to thank all the teachers and educators of the world. My mom worked tirelessly at her craft. She loved science – learning about it, teaching it. She lived it.

One more shoutout to Kay Olayinka, the graphic artist who designed the amazing, thought-provoking cover for this book. You really captured the essence of the story.

And a hearty thanks to David Little-Smith for the back cover photo and Jonathan Holloway for the inside cover photo.

And lastly, to my friend and editor, Izzy Findlay. Thank you for your hard work, insight, and expertise in helping me find my voice and fulfill this dream.

To everyone I mentioned, I love you.

And if you're reading this, I love you, too.

–JB

ABOUT THE AUTHOR

John Bush is a professional drummer and percussionist, originally from Dallas, Texas. He is best known for his role as a founding member of the platinum-selling band, Edie Brickell & New Bohemians. John has been writing stories since he was a child. When he started putting lyrics to his own music, he stopped writing short stories. His songs became his storytelling. Currently, he's penning several pieces of fiction, as well as a collection of non-fiction stories. When he's not writing, John enjoys going to baseball games with his son, Elec, and thrift store shopping with his daughter, Livvy. He's also fond of road trips, playing disc golf, and camping. John lives in Austin, Texas – the "Live Music Capital of the World" – where he performs in several groups. He's been fortunate to have traveled the world playing and recording music. John works regularly as a session musician and has his own studio, Cicada Moon Studios, where he produces music with other artists.